"Oh, Chris. We've got company."

Snort, snort. Sputter, sputter.

"He's beautiful, and you can see right through him."

I swear, if you're talking about men Chris will hear you even in her sleep. Her eyes popped open. Then she let out the kind of yelp I'd managed to avoid so far.

The ghost looked startled. An instant later he was gone. But before he faded out of sight he took a moment to do something wonderful. Sweeping off his hat, he made a deep bow. Then he put his fingers to his lips—and blew us a kiss.

Chris clapped her hands over her heart. "I think I'm in love. . . ."

THE
GHOST WORE
GRAY

Bruce Coville

BANTAM BOOKS
NEW YORK · TORONTO · LONDON · SYDNEY · AUCKLAND

For Cynthia

RL 5, 008–012

THE GHOST WORE GRAY
A Bantam Skylark Book / August 1988

*Skylark Books is a registered trademark of Bantam Books,
a division of Bantam Doubleday Dell Publishing Group, Inc.
Registered in U.S. Patent and Trademark Office and elsewhere.*

ISBN 0-553-15610-1

Published simultaneously in the United States and Canada

*Bantam Books are published by Bantam Books, a division of Bantam
Doubleday Dell Publishing Group, Inc. Its trademark, consisting of the
words "Bantam Books" and the portrayal of a rooster, is Registered in
U.S. Patent and Trademark Office and in other countries. Marca Regis-
trada. Bantam Books, 1540 Broadway, New York, New York 10036.*

PRINTED IN THE UNITED STATES OF AMERICA

OPM   21 20 19 18 17 16 15

CONTENTS

CHAPTER ONE

The Quackadoodle

"Sigh."

That was me, Nina Tanleven.

"I know. Double sigh."

That was my best friend, Chris Gurley. We were lying on the floor of Chris's bedroom, looking at magazines and being depressed.

"Does everyone feel like this when a play ends?" I asked. Chris and I had been acting in a show being done at one of the local theaters that summer. Now that it was over, life seemed incredibly boring.

"I don't know," said Chris. She rolled a strand of reddish blond hair through her fingers and pulled it over her nose. "I'd look it up, but I'm too depressed."

"I wish we could do another one," I said wistfully. "I wouldn't even complain about rehearsals."

"You have to complain about rehearsals. It's traditional. Anyway, what I really miss are the people."

I knew what she meant. While we were working on *The Woman in White* the rest of the

1

cast had become like a second family. Now there was no reason for us to get together anymore.

Except for Chris and me. When we met at the auditions, the two of us had become friends almost instantly. We moved from "just friends" to "best friends" when we teamed up to solve the mystery behind the ghost haunting the Grand Theater where the play was being produced. Despite the fact that we go to different schools, we plan to be best friends forever.

We were still lying there feeling sorry for ourselves when Chris's mother poked her head into the room. "Come on, Nine. I'll drive you home."

I sighed again and got up. "See you later," I said to Chris.

She flopped her hand listlessly. "See you later."

We both sighed.

You'd think that when someone is that depressed, the people around them would have the good manners to be a little depressed, too. Not *my* father. When Mrs. Gurley dropped me off, I dragged myself into the house, only to find Dad dancing around the kitchen, playing a tune on the pots and pans. Now Dad's a little weird, even at his best. But when I saw this act, I began to wonder if he had finally flipped for real.

"This is it, kid!" he yelled when he spotted me in the doorway. Making a lunge in my direction, he swooped me up and began swinging me around in a huge circle.

"What's going on?" I shrieked.

"I got the commission! This is it—the big break!"

"Dad, that's fantastic!"

"I know," he said smugly.

My father is a preservation architect, which means he takes crummy old buildings that used to be beautiful and tries to make them beautiful again. He works for one of the best firms in Syracuse, New York. But for a long time he's been wanting to go out on his own. "Oh, Nine," he would moan when we were having supper. "I want to burst the bonds of employment, shatter the shackles of salary, dump the daily drudge—"

"Yeah, I know," I would say. "You want to be a bum."

Actually, I only said that to tease him. My father works very hard. But he'd much rather be working for himself. For one thing, he has his own ideas about how to do things. They sound great to me. But when you're working for someone else, you usually have to do things their way.

That's why I plan on owning my own business when I grow up.

"So you got the job," I said when he finally put me down. "Is it being too nosy if I ask which one?"

"THE job," said Dad. "The plum I've been trying to pluck for months now. The assignment that will get my name in major design magazines across the country."

"Oh, that job," I said.

He smiled.

"Well, which one is it?" I finally shouted.

"The Quackadoodle."

"Say that again?"

"The Quackadoodle," he repeated.

"What's a Quackadoodle do?" I asked.

"Very funny, twit," he said. "It doesn't do anything. It just sits there."

"Sort of like Sidney?" I asked.

Sidney is our cat. He's big, orange, and lazy. If you see him from the wrong angle, it's easy to get confused and think he's a pillow.

"No, not like Sidney," said Dad. "The Quackadoodle is an inn. A very old inn, located in the Catskill Mountains. A very *run-down* old inn that is going to be incredibly beautiful when I get done with it!"

A sudden thought struck me.

"When did you get this news?" I asked.

"About three hours ago."

"And have you done anything I ought to know about since then?"

He looked at me, the picture of wounded innocence. "Me?" he asked sweetly.

Ever since my mother left two years ago, I've kind of felt it was my job to keep my father from doing things without thinking. But sometimes he moves pretty fast. I had a feeling this was one of those times.

I looked him straight in the eye. "Dad?"

"Yes?" he said, acting as if this were a brand-new conversation.

"Should I be nervous?"

"Are you kidding?" he said. "When you're living with Henry Tanleven, the number one free-lance preservation architect in Syracuse?"

"I knew it!" I yelled. "I knew it. You quit your job. We'll be living on the street and eating bread crusts within three months."

Actually, I didn't believe that for a minute. In fact, I was secretly very happy. My father is really talented. He *should* be working for himself. But I didn't want him to take this too lightly.

"Nine," he said. "You wound me. Anyway, I took this job partly for you."

I looked at him suspiciously—which is the best tactic to take anytime adults tell you they're doing something for your sake. "What do you mean?"

My father smiled. "I just thought Syracuse's number one ghost buster might enjoy spending the rest of the summer at a haunted inn."

CHAPTER TWO

Patience

"Will you come to my funeral?" asked Chris.

We were leaning against a monument in Oakwood Cemetery, which is this enormous graveyard about a mile from my house. It's a good place for being alone. We were at our favorite spot, a huge tree we duck under for shelter when the sun gets too hot.

"When are you having it?" I asked, popping the head off a dandelion. "I don't like to make plans more than fifty years in advance, you know."

Chris bounced an acorn off a nearby tombstone. "Probably about a week and a half from now."

I stopped picking dandelions and looked at her. "What," I asked sternly, "are you talking about?"

"Boredom—which is what I'm going to die of after you go." She began sliding down the side of a monument that was right by the tree. "It's starting to happen already! I see a light, Nine! A light at the end of a long, dark tunnel!"

Three seconds later she was stretched out flat on the ground. She reached over, picked up one of my discarded dandelions, and laid it on her chest.

"Ah-hoo," she said weakly.

"Ah-hoo?" I asked.

"It's the sound someone makes when they die of boredom."

I dropped my dandelions on her face. "You think this stupid inn is going to be fun?" I asked. "I bet there won't be anybody there but old people in their forties. I won't know anyone. I'll be cut off from my home and my friends. But is anyone worried about me? Oh, no! Does anyone wonder how I'm going to do, all alone out there in the boondocks? Oh, no! Does anyone—"

"But a ghost!" cried Chris, jumping up and brushing off her jeans. "It's got a ghost. I can't believe it. Your father has a job at a haunted inn! Some people have all the luck."

"It's just an old story," I said, trying to sound like I wasn't really excited.

"Yeah—like the ghost in the Grand Theater was just an old story. What kind of ghost is it, anyway?"

"I don't know. Dad just said the inn was rumored to be haunted. I think he only told me so I wouldn't complain too much about going. Anyway, I wish you could come, too."

I stopped talking and stared into the distance. "Hold on," I whispered. "I think I'm about to be brilliant. Would your parents let you come with us?"

"Probably," Chris said. "They're always glad to get one of us out of their hair for a while."

I could understand that. The Gurleys have a huge family. Chris is the only girl, so visiting her is a little like taking a field trip to the YMCA. Or the monkey house at the zoo.

"OK, when you get home tonight try to talk them into it."

"What good will that do? Your father's the one who counts. And I doubt he's going to want me hanging around for three weeks."

"Sure he will," I said. Actually, I wasn't as confident as I sounded. But I thought if I worked it right I wouldn't have to talk him into it at all.

I started at suppertime.

"Something wrong with the cooking?" asked my father as he watched me shove a carrot back and forth across my plate.

"No," I said quietly. "The cooking's fine." It was, too. Except for the nights when he gets too adventurous, my father's really good in the kitchen.

"Well, if it's not the food, it must be the company," he said. "Sorry I'm boring you."

"Oh, it's not that," I said.

He put down his fork. "OK, Nine. What's up?"

"Nothing."

He tightened the corners of his mouth. "I've seen rocks with more enthusiasm for life than you're showing at the moment."

"Are you going to be very busy while we're at this inn?" I asked.

"Of course," he said. "It's a big project for me."

"Oh. Well, will I see much of you?"

"I expect so," he said, although he sounded a little less certain of himself.

"Will there be many kids there?"

He started to answer me, then stopped. "I'm not sure."

"That's OK," I said. "I was just wondering. Can I be excused? I have to start packing."

I walked slowly away from the table. Then I went in my room, closed the door, and looked at the clock. Six-thirty. I wondered how long it would take. I remembered Cute Edgar, the director of *The Woman in White,* telling me that one of the great secrets of acting was planting a seed in the audience's mind and then letting it grow by itself.

"Your problem, Nine," he added "is that once you plant the seed, you go overboard with the fertilizer."

Except he didn't say fertilizer.

At seven forty-three my father came through. "Listen, Nine," he said, poking his head into my room, "I've been thinking. I'm going to be awfully busy while we're at the Quackadoodle. Do you suppose Chris might like to come along to keep you company?"

I jumped off my bed with a whoop and gave him a hug. When he left I grabbed my phone and called Chris. "Start packing!" I yelled. "We leave at eight-thirty Wednesday morning!"

About ten minutes later Dad poked his head into the room again. "You know," he said, "you could have just asked." Sometimes I wonder who's fooling who around here.

CHAPTER THREE

How to Pack

"OK, Sidney," I said, "time to move."

I scooped our cat off my underwear and dumped him onto the floor. Sidney gave my leg a halfhearted whack with his paw, made his cranky sound, and stalked out of my room, twitching his tail angrily.

"That," said Chris, "is one weird cat." She was sitting at the head of my bed, helping me pack, which in this case meant rolling her eyes whenever she considered a piece of clothing too hideous for words.

"Ten minutes!" yelled my father from the living room.

"Ten minutes," I muttered. "I can't possibly be ready in ten minutes!"

"You had all last week," Chris said quietly.

"Don't *you* start on me," I snapped.

What Chris had said was true, of course. But I was already feeling sorry for myself because I had realized that while my father is good at a whole lot of things a mother usually does, helping me get ready for a trip is not one of them. I was also feeling a little silly, because I realized it was no big deal, and guilty, because I knew I was going to make us late. Also cranky, because I really didn't want Chris to watch me pack.

"I think I'll go talk to Sidney," said Chris. "He's in a better mood."

I waited until she was gone, then sighed in relief. Now I could get started! Using what I call the grab-and-stuff method, I snatched up the pile of underwear and threw it in the suitcase. Socks, shirts, jeans, and T-shirts came next. A couple of sweaters, a few good skirts and blouses, and I was just about finished.

It's a very efficient system, but not the kind of thing you particularly want someone else to watch. I almost made it, too. I was just trying to close the lid when Chris came back into the room. "Good grief," she said, when she saw the stack of clothes being squashed into the suitcase.

"Be quiet and help me push," I said. She got on the other corner of the suitcase. Between the two of us we managed to get it closed and fastened.

"Uh-oh," said Chris.

The cuff of a red sweater was sticking out on the right side.

"Forget it," I said. "Getting it in now would be more trouble than it's worth."

"The Golden Chariot awaits," called my father. The Golden Chariot is what Dad likes to call his car, which is this ancient 1964 Cadillac he bought when I was a little kid. It's yellow and white. It has huge fins. And it's longer than almost every parking space in town. It also breaks down at least once a month, but Dad claims the repair bills are no worse than the car payments most people make. He says its worth it to have a car with class.

I think it makes sense for a preservation architect to have a car like that. It's like the buildings he loves—big, old, and kind of funky.

Chris had ridden in the Chariot several times. But she still wasn't prepared for how much room we had in the trunk. After Dad opened it, she stood looking inside for a moment then said, with awe in her voice, "You know, if you put in plumbing, you could rent that out as an apartment."

Like I said, it's a big car.

Since I believe in first things first, my box of books was already in the trunk. Dad's tennis racket and golf clubs lay next to them.

"Hey, Mr. T," said Chris, "I thought this was a working trip."

"It's an experiment," I said. "He hasn't played golf in seven years."

"I am ignoring you both," said my father, throwing in the last of the suitcases. He went back into the house. A minute later he came out with the cat carrier. Sidney was inside, complaining mightily.

"Is he coming with us?" asked Chris.

"He's staying with my grandmother," I said.

"Lucky Gramma," said Chris, climbing into the backseat of the Chariot. I climbed in next to her.

Dad started the car.

"Are we almost there?" I teased when we got to the end of the block.

"Did I tell you I found a kennel that takes kids?" replied Dad.

I decided to be quiet for a while. It was four hours before I asked that same question again, and this time I was serious. I was sick of riding. Dad glanced at his watch, and at the map beside him. "Another hour and a half," he said, "assuming Baltimore's directions are accurate."

"Baltimore?" asked Chris.

"Baltimore Cleveland," said Dad. "The man who owns the Quackadoodle."

"You really know a human being named Baltimore Cleveland?" I asked.

He glanced over his shoulder. "Not only do I know him, but he's going to be our host for the next three weeks. And he's going to be paying me a lot of money."

"It's a wonderful name," I said. "Just wonderful. I think I'll look at the scenery for a while."

The scenery was worth looking at. Steep, rocky hills covered with pines stretched up to our right. Little streams splashed and bounced down these same hills, then disappeared under the road, only to pop up on the other side, where they meandered off through the more gentle ter-

ritory that sloped away in that direction. It reminded me of pictures I had seen of England.

"It won't be that much farther now," announced my father as he turned the Golden
Chariot onto a narrow, winding road. Dad's idea
of not much farther is different from my own,
but eventually we saw a sign that said
"Quackadoodle Inn—3 miles."

Eventually we saw the inn itself.

Dad stopped the car. He stared at the inn
with a kind of glazed expression on his face. I
couldn't tell if he was struck with a vision of
what the place could be—or appalled by what it
looked like right then.

"Well, Mr. Tanleven," said Chris cheerfully,
"it looks like you've got your work cut out for
you."

Dad's dream project was a rambling old
three-story building, surrounded by a wide
porch cluttered with big wooden chairs. The top
of the inn was a strange jumble of towers, tur-
rets, dormers, and cupolas.

It was fascinating. But it was also a mess.
The porch was sagging, the roof was mossy, and
the walls were marked by dark spots where
shingles had fallen away.

I shivered. I had never seen a place that
looked more likely to be haunted.

CHAPTER FOUR

Baltimore Cleveland

The lobby was empty.

"Hello?" called my father, juggling two suit-cases, a tennis racket, and golf clubs.

"Be right with you!" yelled someone in another room.

"That's Baltimore," my father said. "I recognize his voice."

We put down our suitcases and looked around.

The fading purple wallpaper was covered with huge red flowers. The threadbare oriental carpet had seen better days—and probably better years. The antique furniture was heavy and dark, and looked as if it had been selected to prove one of my father's favorite sayings: "Just because something is old, it doesn't necessarily follow that it's beautiful."

I looked at Chris. She looked at me. We rolled our eyes. But before either of us could say anything, a round little man came bustling into the room. "Good morning, good morning!" he cried, ignoring the fact that it was well past

15

noon. "You must be the Tanlevens. I'm Baltimore Cleveland." He thrust out his arm and
began pumping my father's hand.

Chris and I tried to keep from giggling. Baltimore Cleveland looked a little like a creature
from a fairy tale. He was about five feet tall (I
know because I'm four foot ten, and he was only
an inch or so taller than me). His cheeks were as
round and as red as a pair of apples. He had
twinkling blue eyes with those little crinkles at
the sides you always see on people who spend
most of their time smiling. His eyebrows were
bushy and white, matching the thick fringe of
white hair that circled his otherwise bald head.
He wore an apron that had once been white, but
was now decorated with bits of food of almost
every imaginable color. A smudge of flour whit-
ened the tip of his nose.

Dad got his hand free from Mr. Cleveland's
grasp and turned toward Chris and me.

"This is my daughter, Nine, and her friend,
Chris Gurley."

"Nine?" asked the innkeeper, giving me a
funny look.

"Well, it's really Nina. But everyone calls
me Nine, because of my last name."

He looked puzzled.

"You know, Nine Tan-leven?" I asked, hoping he would get it without any more explanation.

He narrowed his eyes, and then his bushy
white eyebrows popped up in surprise. "Oh, I
see!" he cried in delight. "Very good. Very good,

indeed! Well, I'll call you Nine, and you can call
me Baltimore. Or Balty, although I don't particularly like that, since it sounds too much like
Baldy."

"I'll call you Baltimore," I said, shaking his
pudgy hand.

When he had pumped Chris's hand to his
satisfaction, Baltimore led us out of the lobby
into a wide hall that ended at the foot of a long
staircase. I glanced at my father and saw him
cringe as he took in the wallpaper. The only
thing in the hall that looked good was a huge
batch of fresh-cut flowers, sitting in a glass vase
on a table set against one wall.

Following Baltimore, we walked up the
creaking stairway and then down another long
hall decorated with a dozen or so framed pictures. To my surprise, about half of them were
fairly good. A group of old photographs caught
my attention. I made a mental note to take a
closer look at them when I had a chance.

"And here are your rooms," Baltimore announced, stopping at a pair of doors that stood
side by side. "This is for Poppa," he said, swinging open one door. "And this is for the young
ladies."

"See you later, kids," said Dad. He stepped
into his room. I stepped into ours, hoping it
wasn't covered with the kind of wallpaper that
would make me want to skip breakfast. Chris
was right behind me. "Hey," she said. "Not bad."

She was right. To my surprise, the room was
almost pretty. It had two brass beds with white

coverlets, a desk, a dresser, two battered but comfortable-looking armchairs, and lacy curtains that moved slowly in the breeze. The wallpaper was a simple design of pink and blue stripes.

"Dibs on this one," said Chris, throwing her suitcase on the bed nearest the window. I thought about fighting her for it, then decided I should let her have it since she was my guest. I watched as she suddenly turned, realizing that maybe she should have waited for me to choose. "Unless you want it," she said.

I shook my head. "You'll probably catch cold there, anyway," I said.

"Your closet is here," said Baltimore, pointing to the only other door in the room. "Your bathroom is the third door on the right as you're heading back to the stairs."

"We don't have one of our own?" I asked in shock.

Baltimore shook his head. "This is a very old inn," he said with a smile. "It was a big deal when they brought the plumbing indoors. That was back in—"

He was interrupted by a screeching voice from the top of the stairs. "Baltimore! Baltimore Cleveland! I want to see you this moment!"

"My wife," said Baltimore with a sigh. "I'd better find out what she wants. You girls have a pleasant afternoon. I'll see you at dinner."

"Baltimore!" screeched the voice again.

"Coming, Gloria," called the innkeeper. He bustled off down the hall, wiping his hands on his apron.

Chris looked at me and we both burst out laughing. "Baltimore!" she cried, doing a perfect imitation of the screeching Gloria. "Baltimore Cleveland, you come here right now!"

"Shhh!" I hissed, closing the door and sagging against the wall. "She might hear you."

We giggled our way through unpacking, first dividing the dresser and the closet equally. I put my stack of books next to my bed, then went to stand at the window.

"Nice view," said Chris, coming to stand beside me.

She was right. Our window looked out onto the inn's backyard, which was small and neatly trimmed, with a scattering of wooden chairs. The yard was bordered by a stream, about six feet wide, that bounced and bubbled over glistening rocks. The midday sunshine made the water sparkle as though it were filled with diamonds. A little footbridge crossed the stream about fifty feet from our window. The bridge led to a path that disappeared into the forest.

We were just deciding to go and explore when my father stuck his head into the room.

"How are you two doing?" he asked.

"Great," I said. "Do you mind if we go out for a walk?"

He glanced at his watch. "No problem. But if you can make it back in ninety minutes, Baltimore is going to be giving me a tour of the inn. I thought you might like to come along. It's a fascinating old place."

"Sounds good to me," I said, glancing at Chris. She nodded.

"Fine," said Dad. "I'll meet you in the lobby."

"Are you sure your heart can stand it?" I asked.

He laughed. "It really is horrible, isn't it? I'll just be sure to take a lot of before-and-after photos. Even if I only do a halfway decent job, people will think I'm a genius when they see what the place used to look like. See you guys in an hour and a half."

He popped back into his room. Chris and I headed out into the hallway, where I remembered the old photographs I had spotted on the way in.

"Stop a minute," I said. "I want to look at these."

The five pictures were arranged in a kind of X-shape: two above, two below, and one in the center. Each was in a fancy, gold-painted wooden frame.

They were all interesting, but it was the one in the center that held my attention. It was a picture of a man in a Confederate Army uniform. I've seen other photos from the Civil War period, and while the men are OK, they're not what I'd call gorgeous. That wasn't the case here. This was a picture of one of the most handsome men I had ever seen. He was staring intently at the camera, as people usually did in those old photos. But the serious look in his large, dark eyes was offset by a smile that tugged at the corners of his mouth—as if he couldn't really imagine being *that* serious for long. The gray uniform accented his broad shoulders and trim waist, and there was something exciting about the way his hand rested on the saber at his side.

Chris sighed. "What a hunk. Too bad he's dead."

That was when it happened.

I shivered and looked at Chris. She was already looking at me.

"Did you feel that?" she whispered.

I nodded. Frozen in place, I turned my head ever so slightly and rolled my eyes to the side so I could look over my shoulder.

There was no one there—no one who could have laid an ice-cold hand on the back of my neck.

But I had felt it. And so had Chris.

"Come on," she said. "Let's get out of here!"

We got.

CHAPTER FIVE

The Secret Cemetery

"Hunk alert," whispered Chris.

"I don't think I can take it," I said. "I'm still recovering from the hunk in the hallway."

"Well, this one is alive and well and standing about thirty feet to your left."

We were in the backyard of the Quackadoodle, still trying to figure out if what had happened in the hallway was just a trick of our imaginations. I decided to put the question on hold and check out the action on the left.

Chris was right. The tall blond slapping green paint on one of the wooden chairs was definitely alive and well. He looked up and smiled at us. "Hi, girls," he said, waving his paintbrush.

I felt myself begin to blush.

He put down the paintbrush and ambled in our direction. "Are you staying here?" he asked.

I nodded.

"Good. I think you'll like it. Baltimore's a good host. But watch out for Gloria. She's—"

Before he could finish the sentence, a shrill voice came arrowing out of an upstairs window. "Peter! Peter Gorham! You get back to work!"

Peter winked at us. "Speak of the devil," he whispered. "I'd better go paint. Stop and chat with me later if you feel like it."

It took all my willpower to keep from reaching out to push back the curl of blond hair that had fallen down over his forehead.

"We'll probably do that," said Chris.

"Peter!" cried the voice from the window.

"Yes, ma'am!" he yelled. "Right away." He dropped his voice. "See you later," he whispered as he headed back to his job.

"I don't get it," I said when we stopped on the footbridge to watch the water chuckle along. "Why would a guy who looks like that, and who has to be at least nineteen, bother with the two of us?"

"Speak for yourself!" said Chris. "I may be only eleven, but I'm irresistible to men."

"So are potato chips," I said. "And dips, which you happen to be if you think you're ready to knock any man over fourteen off his feet."

She shrugged. "Maybe we're the only girls here. Maybe he just likes to gossip. Or maybe it was my hazel eyes."

"You can't see hazel eyes from where we were standing," I pointed out. "I vote for boredom."

"Well, I vote we keep walking if we're going to see anything before we have to meet your father," she answered.

We crossed the bridge and entered the forest. Between the shadows and the silence, the place seemed almost magical. It was warm and lazy. Shafts of brightness struck down through the trees, making puddles of gold on the scatterings of last year's leaves. The air smelled of pine trees, damp soil, and something else that I couldn't quite place, but which seemed rich and alive. It reminded me of the places I used to see in my head when my mother read me fairy tales.

"I love it," whispered Chris.

I nodded. But I didn't speak. I felt it was somehow improper to say too much in this place.

We wandered on, following the path through the trees. Sometimes it bordered the stream, sometimes it veered away so we couldn't see the sparkle of the water. But we could always hear it rushing along off to our right.

The path made a wide loop and began to struggle its way up a hill. The sound of the moving water became faint for a while. Then, as we circled back, it grew louder again. Before long it was no longer a burble but a roar. I thought I knew what that meant. So I was delighted, but not too surprised, when the path took us around a tall rock and we found ourselves standing at the top of a beautiful waterfall.

"What a spot for a moonlight stroll," said Chris. She was standing on one of the large rocks that edged the falls, gazing down to where the stream tumbled into a foaming pool some thirty or forty feet below.

"Yeah, and I know who you'd like to go strolling with," I said.

We dawdled by the waterfall for a while, until I noticed a very faint path leading off to the right. It didn't look as though anyone had used it for some time.

"Let's see where this goes," I said.

To our surprise, it led to a tiny cemetery.

The graveyard was in a clearing, or what had once been a clearing; now it was starting to fill in with small trees and shrubs again. Fifteen or twenty old tombstones dotted the area. Flowering vines crawled over many of the taller stones, and the grass was so high that some of the shorter markers could hardly be seen. I wondered if other, even smaller stones had been completely covered by the grass. The idea seemed sad to me.

We stood at the edge of the cemetery for a moment. Then Chris picked up a stick and walked over to the nearest tombstone. Pushing aside the prickly canes of an old-fashioned rose, she revealed the words underneath: "Martha Ives—1871 to 1882."

"Eleven years old," she said. "The same as us."

I took a deep breath. We wandered around and read the other stones. Most of them seemed to have come from the 1870s and 1880s. The only exception was a tall stone at the far side of the cemetery. When we pushed aside the vines to read the inscription this is what we found.

Jonathan Gray

Captain in the Confederate Army

Born 1837

Died 1863

Erected in Loving Memory by His
Many Friends

1875

I looked at Chris. "Confederate Army. Do you suppose that could be the guy whose picture is hanging in the inn?" I asked.

Before she could answer, something happened that pretty much answered my question.

I felt an icy hand brush against my neck.

"Come on!" I said. Grabbing Chris by the hand, I headed for the path. From the look in her eyes I didn't have to explain. She had felt the same thing.

We raced back past the waterfall and into the woods. It was only when we were about halfway back to the inn and had stopped to catch our breath that I remembered we were supposed to meet my father and Baltimore for a tour. I had a feeling we were pretty late, so we started to run again.

Dad was standing on the porch studying his watch when Chris and I came rushing around the corner of the inn. He looked at me and raised an eyebrow.

"Sorry," I gasped. "We went for a walk in the woods and lost track of the time."

He nodded and walked back into the building.

"Is he mad?" asked Chris nervously.

"I don't think so," I said. "Not unless we're later than I think. He just wants me to know I goofed up."

I could see her relax a little. "You're lucky," she said. "My father doesn't believe in silent messages."

When we went into the lobby we found Baltimore and my father talking. Actually, Baltimore was doing the talking. My father was listening to the little man, who at one point actually flapped his arms as though he were about to take off. He turned when he heard us enter.

"Hello, hello!" he cried as though he hadn't seen us for days. "Are you all set for the grand tour?"

"Can't wait," I said. "I love old buildings."

"I see you've trained her well," said Baltimore, winking at my father. I started to object—calling me "trained" made me feel like a dog. But Baltimore had already jumped into his presentation.

"The first Quackadoodle was built in 1805," he said, his white eyebrows waggling. "Unfortunately, it burned to the ground in 1806. The second was built in 1807. It lasted twenty years before fire got it, too. The third inn was put up in 1833. That's the building we're standing in now—or at least part of it. There have been a lot of additions over the years."

Baltimore led us out of the lobby, through the hall with the stairway, and into a large room filled with tables. A stone fireplace took up most of the wall to our left. "The Quackadoodle dining room," said Baltimore proudly. Two women were hurrying around the room, preparing it for dinner. One of them was setting out silverware and straightening the white linen tablecloths. The other was putting pink flowers into small white vases.

Baltimore raised his voice. "Martha," he called. "Isabella! I want you to meet some special guests."

The women looked up. The woman with the flowers was named Isabella. She was very pretty, with dark skin and dark eyes that seemed to have something hidden inside them. Martha, the woman with the silverware, looked as cold and sharp as the knives she was holding. She was much older than Isabella—somewhere in her midfifties was my father's guess, when I asked him later.

Baltimore introduced us and told the women not to be concerned if they saw my father poking around in odd places. He would have to do that as part of his planning for the renovation. I noticed Isabella's eyes widen when Baltimore mentioned why my father was there. *That's odd,* I thought to myself. *I wonder why she's so interested.* I made a note to talk to Chris about it later.

"Let me show you the kitchen," said Baltimore. He led us through the dining room, which had beautiful windows looking out onto the forest. But the wallpaper should have been arrested for attacking people's eyes.

A pair of swinging doors led into the kitchen. Just as Baltimore was about to push on one of them, the other flew open and Peter Gorham came barreling out as if there were a demon on his tail.

"*Schweinhund!*" cried an angry voice on the far side of the door. "*Dumbkopf!* Imbecile!" I heard a dull thwacking sound. The cursing stopped.

Baltimore grabbed the edge of the door and pulled it open, using it as a shield. Peering around the edge, he found himself face to face with an enormous knife.

CHAPTER SIX

The Unexpected Guest

"Dieter!" bellowed Baltimore. "How many times do I have to tell you not to throw things at the help?"

He pulled the blade out of the door and walked into the kitchen. "Come on," he said, sticking his bald head back around the door into the dining room. "I want you to meet our cook, Dieter Schwartz." (Dieter might seem like a funny name for a cook. But you don't say it the way it looks; it rhymes with "Peter.")

I looked at my father. He shrugged and followed Baltimore. Chris and I stayed close at his heels. I glanced at the back of the door as we went through. It had dozens of knife marks in it.

Dieter Schwartz was actually shorter than Baltimore Cleveland. His face, which seemed to be mostly nose, was red with anger. He stood beside a big pot, scooping something out of it with a ladle, then slapping the ladle back in. He had a disgusted look on his face, and a steady stream of angry German curses was coming out of his mouth. "Dolt!" he cried, switching to English. "I asked him to stir this, and look at it. *Look at it!*"

He held up a spoonful of the stuff. It looked like a combination of silly putty and gravel, only thicker.

"What is it?" Baltimore asked.

"Cream sauce!" bellowed Dieter as though someone had stabbed him through the heart. Then, more weakly, he repeated, "Cream sauce."

Baltimore shook his head sympathetically. "Looks pretty bad," he said. "But I've told you Peter's no cook. That's not what I hired him for."

"I cannot do everything!" cried Dieter. "I must have more help."

Baltimore looked a little nervous. "We'll talk about that later, Dieter. Right now, I want you to meet some special guests."

You would have sworn he had pulled some kind of lever inside Dieter Schwartz's head; although we had been standing right in front of him, he seemed to see us for the first time.

"How pleased I am to make your acquaintance," he said to each of us, as Baltimore introduced us. "You must forgive my little tantrum. I treat my food as an artist treats his paintings, and I cannot bear to have it destroyed like this." He gestured tragically toward the pot of putty. "I fear you have formed a bad impression of me. Ah! I know what will help. Here, try one of these!"

He rushed to the far side of the kitchen and came back with a pastry in each hand. He gave one to me and one to Chris.

I thanked him.

"Eat! Eat!" he cried, waving his hands in the air.

I took a bite.

You can forgive a lot in a man who can make something that tastes like that.

"It's wonderful!" said Chris.

"Yes, I know," said Dieter, putting his hands behind his back and rising up on his tiptoes. "I am a genius."

My father was looking longingly at the pastry in my hand. I was just about to offer him a bite when we were interrupted by a familiar shriek. "Baltimore! Baltimore Cleveland! You come here this minute."

Baltimore sighed. "I guess the rest of our tour will have to wait," he said. "Gloria wants me for something." He handed my father the tube he had been carrying. "Here are the old floor plans I promised you. Dinner's at seven. I'll see you then."

"It was *supposed* to be at seven," said Dieter, looking gloomily at his ruined cream sauce. "Now, I don't know."

"Baltimore!"

The innkeeper winced. "Coming, dear." He turned toward us. "Seven o'clock," he said. Then he hurried off.

"Well," said my father, nodding at the tempermental cook, "I guess we'd better be going, too."

"Go, go!" cried Dieter, turning back to the stove. "I must create! I want dinner tonight to please the young ladies!"

Dad gestured toward the door with his head, and we followed him out of the kitchen.

Martha and Isabella were just finishing up in the dining room. "Lucky you," said Isabella, when she saw the goodies Chris and I were carrying. "Dieter doesn't pass those out to just anyone."

"Obviously," said my father in a mournful voice. I laughed and handed him my pastry. He took a bite, then laid his hand over his heart. "Ruined!" he cried. "I'll never eat another sweet again without remembering this glorious moment." He looked at it greedily. "Are you sure you want it back?"

"Positive," I said, taking it out of his hand.

"I'll tell Dieter you liked it," said Isabella. "He'll be pleased."

Martha snorted, which seemed to be the extent of her vocabulary.

"Well," said Chris, slipping a blue dress over her head, "I think we're in for an interesting three weeks."

I nodded in agreement. I would have answered out loud, but I was holding my brush in my mouth while I tried to work an elastic band over my hair.

There was a knock at our door. "Ready?" called my father.

I spit the brush onto my bed. "Just a minute," I yelled. I turned my back to Chris. "Button me," I said.

Sixty seconds later we presented ourselves to my father, who looked us over approvingly. "Very nice," he said. "It's not every man who gets to go to dinner with two such lovely ladies."

We giggled and took his arms to walk down the hall. I braced myself as we passed the old

photographs, but there was no repetition of the
cold chill I had felt earlier that day.

Baltimore was waiting for us at the entrance to the dining room. "I decided to make
dinner a bit of an occasion tonight," he said. "We
sometimes do this midweek, when there aren't
too many guests."

Looking past him, I saw that some of the
tables had been pushed together to create a
large table in the center of the room. I did a
quick plate count. It was set for ten. Three of the
chairs were already filled—two by a pleasant-
looking older couple, the third by a very good-
looking younger woman.

The pretty woman turned out to be an editor from New York City. Her name was Mona
Curtis. She had dark hair, enormous brown
eyes, and long fingers. She also had a thing for
my father. He didn't notice it, of course. He's
pretty dense about that kind of thing. But I
spotted it the minute they were introduced.
Maybe it's just something one woman can tell
about another. It's not the first time it's happened. I mean, my father is not a bad-looking
guy. The thing is, he doesn't know it. In fact, he
generally doesn't notice when a woman is interested in him, unless she just about hits him over
the head.

This is a problem, mostly because it makes
him an easy target for the kind of woman who
doesn't mind hitting a guy over the head. That
made Mona's presence at dinner depressing; I

get nervous when I see a woman about to sink her claws into my father.

The older man and woman were a retired couple visiting from Canada. "Mr. and Mrs. Arnold Coleman," said Baltimore, making the formal introduction.

"Please, please," said Mr. Coleman, pushing back his chair and standing up to greet us. "Call us Arnie and Meg. We'll be much more comfortable that way."

Arnie was as tall as Baltimore was short—"six foot five," he told me later when I got up the courage to ask him. He had a head of thick, white hair, and that kind of leathery look that usually means a person has spent most of his or her life outdoors. Meg was small and cuddly. She made me think of the women who serve the church dinners I go to with my grandmother.

"Well," said Baltimore. "As soon as my wife and Mr. Markson arrive, we can begin."

I counted the seats again. "Isn't there someone else coming?" I asked.

He shook his head. "I like to set an extra place, just in case. It's an innkeeper's duty. Ah, here's Mr. Markson!"

Baltimore hurried to the door of the dining room, where the newcomer had just appeared. Taking the man by the arm, he steered him to the table and again introduced everyone.

There was an awkward moment when Baltimore introduced my father.

"Ah," said Mr. Markson, "the man who has my room." His voice was quiet but slightly testy.

Baltimore blushed and explained that there had been a mix-up and he had put my dad in the room that was normally reserved for Mr. Markson, who was a longtime customer of the inn.

Dad offered to trade. Mr. Markson made a funny noise and told him not to worry about it, and the tension vanished.

Aside from that instant of crankiness, Porter Markson struck me as being the most average man I'd ever seen—average height, average weight, average looks. His hair was kind of a medium brown, his clothes medium stylish. He seemed nice, but very forgettable.

Gloria Cleveland, on the other hand, was a complete surprise. She appeared at the doorway of the dining room about five minutes after Porter Markson, and it was as if someone had turned on a light. After all the screeching we had heard from her that afternoon, Chris and I had figured she would be some kind of hag.

Some hag! She was tall, blond, and gorgeous. Her dress looked like something from one of the nighttime soaps.

"No wonder he puts up with her," Chris whispered.

And, indeed, Baltimore seemed to glow at the sight of his lovely wife. "Well," he said, rubbing his hands together. "Our little party is finally complete."

As it turned out, he was wrong about that. The last guest didn't show up until we were eating our dessert.

That was when the ghost sat down in the empty chair—directly across from me.

CHAPTER SEVEN

Look Into My Eyes

I was squishing peach melba between my teeth when the ghost showed up. I was so surprised I almost sprayed a mouthful of the stuff all over Mona Curtis. Fortunately, I kept it under control. Disgusted as I was at the way she was drooling over my father, I still knew that a shower of peach-raspberry goo wasn't the way to handle the situation.

I also know that dessert squishing is a disgusting habit. Fortunately, none of the grownups noticed it, mostly because they were so tied up in their own conversations. Besides, it wasn't just habit that night. I was doing it out of frustration. For the last hour and a half, I had been watching Mona circle my father like a vulture circles a wounded rabbit. And I still hadn't been able to figure out any way to warn him about her.

This is not to say that dinner was a total disaster. To begin with, the food was spectacular—even if it was mostly things I had never heard of before. The main dish was some

kind of mystery meat, covered with mushrooms.
But these weren't just ordinary mushrooms. According to Baltimore they were "domestic and
imported, both wild and cultivated." Or something like that. Anyway, I never saw so many
different kinds of mushrooms on one plate.

Then there were the cucumbers. Now I've
been eating cucumbers all my life. You peel
them and slice them, right?

Not Dieter. After peeling them he had cut
them in half the long way and scooped out all
the seeds. Then he sliced them, which made all
the pieces come out like little crescent moons.
Then he *cooked* them. I mean, who ever heard of
cooking cucumbers? Anyway, they were still
firm, and kind of shimmery, and covered with
this clear, shiny sauce.

But it was the peach melba that caused my
mouth to send a message to my brain, asking if
we had died and gone to heaven. That was the
other reason I was squishing it; I wanted to
make it last.

As good as the food was, when I think back
on that meal I remember the sounds almost as
well as the tastes. If I close my eyes I can still
hear the bursts of laughter, the clink of glasses,
the cries of delight as Martha and Isabella de-
livered each new course. The conversation
seemed to whirl around the table, all very witty
and grown-up sounding. The fact that people got
friendly so quickly may have had something to
do with the wine, which was flowing pretty
freely. I think it also had something to do with

ordinary-looking Porter Markson, who turned
out to be a wonderful storyteller.

Porter was also a good source of information, since he had been coming to the Quackadoodle for nearly thirty years. In a way it
seemed as if the place belonged to him more
than it did to Baltimore and Gloria, who had
only bought it two years earlier. Porter told
funny stories about the guests who used to come
there, and a romantic story about two people
who met and fell in love there, and then a sad
story about how beautiful the inn had been before the last owners had let it get so run-down
that most of the old regulars stopped coming
back.

"But here's to our new hosts, Baltimore and
Gloria," he concluded, raising his wineglass for
a toast. "May they bring the Quackadoodle back
to its former glory!"

We all raised our glasses and cheered.
Baltimore was beaming. It was very nice, except
that I thought Porter should have also mentioned my father, who was going to have a lot to
do with bringing glory back to this place.

It was shortly after the toast that the ghost
made his appearance. He drifted in through the
dining room door. And I do mean *through*—
Gloria had closed it behind her when she made
her grand entrance. Taking his time, he crossed
the room to where we were sitting and took his
place at the table as if he had been invited.

I heard Chris drop her spoon. I felt her grab
my elbow at about the time I managed to swal-
low the peach melba. "Do you see it?" she hissed.

I nodded, my eyes wide.

We recognized him at once: he was the same man we had seen in the photo upstairs. He was wearing his uniform, and if it wasn't for the fact that he was dead, I would say he looked even better in real life than he did in the picture.

The adults babbled on, totally unaware of the ghost's presence. Chris and I tried to stay calm, but I could feel my hands begin to tremble. I suppose if we hadn't already had one experience with a ghost we probably would have screamed and jumped out of our seats. As it was, we managed to keep ourselves under control.

As we watched, it became clear that the ghost was slowly and carefully studying the people at the table. He started with Porter Markson, who was sitting to his right, then moved on to Arnie, then Meg, and finally to Baltimore, who was sitting right next to me.

I braced myself, knowing I would be next. When he turned his eyes on me, I looked straight back at him.

I don't know if you've ever looked a ghost in the eye before. We are talking major weird experience here. It wasn't so much what I could see— my memory tells me I was staring into two empty, black holes. It was more like something I *felt*: as if I were falling out of time and into somewhere else altogether. The sensation only lasted for an instant, mostly because several things happened all at once.

One, I was swept by this terrible wave of sorrow.

Two, the ghost broke the eye lock.

And three, he disappeared—just blinked out of sight.

"What did you do to him?" whispered Chris. I think she was angry because he hadn't gotten around to staring at her, too.

"I didn't do anything except look at him," I hissed back. "I think he was surprised that I could see him."

About that time my father shot us his save-the-whispering-for-later look. We shut up and tried to pay attention to the conversation. But both of us were dying for dinner to be over so we could talk about what had happened.

It didn't take that much longer. When Martha and Isabella brought around refills for the coffee, Dad leaned over and asked if we wanted to be excused. Normally we would have hung around for a while, to see if we might hear a couple of juicy jokes. But that night we didn't think anything that might come up at the table would be half as interesting as what we had already seen. So we complimented Baltimore and Gloria on the meal and then took off.

The dining room had doors that opened onto the broad porch which wrapped around the inn. We went out there and settled into a couple of wooden chairs. It was a warm, clear night. The nearly full moon made everything look as if it had been brushed with silver, and the sound of the stream gurgling to itself as it rolled along the far edge of the lawn was soothing. I could smell the water, and just a hint of the fresh paint from the chairs Peter Gorham had covered that afternoon.

We propped our feet up on the porch rail and sat in silence for a moment.

"Well, what do you think?" I asked after a while.

"I think you have all the luck," said Chris.

"Next time I'll pretend I don't see him, so you can have a chance," I snapped. I really didn't want to have a fight with my best friend over a ghost.

Chris smiled. "I'm sorry. Just jealous, I guess."

I smiled back. "I guess I can't blame you. He's gorgeous! But honestly, all I did was look at him."

"Why do you think that surprised him so much?" asked Chris.

"Well, obviously he wasn't expecting anyone to see him."

"OK, so why did we see him?"

"Now that," I said, "is a question worth asking. Unfortunately, I don't have an answer."

"Well then, let me ask you this one," said Chris. "Are we dealing with a good ghost, or a bad ghost?"

I thought back to our experience with the Woman in White. From the beginning, both of us had sensed that there was nothing to fear from that ghost.

It wasn't so simple this time around.

"I don't know," I whispered. It wasn't cold, but I shivered and wrapped my arms around myself. "I really don't know."

CHAPTER EIGHT

Piano in the Parlor

We had been sitting on the porch for about half an hour, looking at the stars and talking about ghosts when Chris suddenly grabbed my arm. "Listen," she hissed. "Do you hear music?"

I cocked my head and listened. The sound was so low it was hard to hear above the splashing of the stream. But it was there all right, the soft, sweet tinkle of a piano drifting out from somewhere in the inn.

I remembered the music we had sometimes heard when the Woman in White was around. "I wonder if it means anything?" I whispered.

"Let's go look!" said Chris.

The dining room was deserted. Even Martha and Isabella were gone, the table already whisked clean of any evidence that people had been eating there just a short time before. Worse, the lights were out. We picked our way through the darkened room, wondering what we would find when we caught up with the music, which was definitely more distinct now that we were inside.

One of the problems with getting involved with ghosts is that after a while you tend to jump at supernatural explanations for things you don't understand, when there may be a perfectly logical reason for what's happening. That was the case now, when the music turned out to be nothing more mysterious than a very solid Porter Markson playing the piano in the parlor.

I guess you'd call it the parlor. It was a room we hadn't seen yet, located on the far side of the lobby. I assume Baltimore would have showed it to us that afternoon, if Gloria hadn't interrupted our tour.

Most of the people who had been at supper were there now, some sitting, some standing at the piano. The only one missing was Meg Coleman. But she came bustling in a few minutes after we did, to take her place next to her towering husband.

My father was sitting on an old sofa. When he saw us he waved his hand to indicate we should come and join him. We did, despite the fact that I was less than thrilled to see Mona perched on the arm of the sofa with one hand resting lightly on his shoulder.

Porter Markson started another song. He was good; I could hardly believe the way his hands flew over the keyboard. He ran through the tune once, then yelled, "Now everybody sing!" I suppose it must have been some old favorite, because everybody but Chris and I knew the words.

"Excuse me a minute," whispered Mona, squeezing my father's shoulder. "I'll be right back."

I curled my lip as I watched her wiggle her way out of the room.

"Nice woman," said Dad appreciatively.

"Yeah," I muttered. "And a tiger is just a nice kitty."

I heard Chris stifle a snort. Dad looked at me and raised an eyebrow, but decided not to comment. Porter started another song. Suddenly Baltimore was in front of us. "Come on," he said, reaching down and pulling on my arm. "Let's all get over by the piano where we belong." He pulled Chris and me to a standing position and then started working on my father.

I suppose it's a host's duty to move a party along. Baltimore did it well. Before long he had everyone standing at the piano and singing. Smiling, he put his arm around Gloria's slender waist. She bent down and planted a kiss on his shiny bald head. How could she be so sweet at night and so ferocious during the day?

We had gone through two more songs before Mona slithered her way back into the room and took her place next to my father. I sighed. She had been gone so long I was beginning to hope maybe she'd poked herself in the eye with her mascara and had to go to bed.

After a while Porter stopped playing and turned around to tell a joke. It was very funny. But I could feel the tips of my ears starting to turn red. My father cleared his throat, and Porter rolled his eyes and made a face that said, "Oops, my mistake!"

I had a feeling the party was nearly over for Chris and me.

"Just when things were starting to get interesting," complained Chris as we began trudging up the stairs. Porter played "Good Night, Ladies," as we were leaving. It was kind of sweet, but a little embarrassing, too. Especially since I had a feeling things were going to get really rowdy once we were gone.

"I wouldn't mind that much, if it wasn't for Mona," I said. "I don't know *what* she'll try without me there to keep an eye on things."

"Hey, you think your father's going to stay a bachelor forever?" asked Chris.

The question stopped me right in my tracks—mostly because I hadn't really thought about it before. I mean, basically it had been just the two of us ever since my mother left. To tell the truth I kind of liked it that way. I guess I assumed Dad did, too, though now that I stopped to consider it, that seemed kind of stupid. I needed time to think about this one.

"Well, what's that got to do with Mona?" I asked, trying to sidestep Chris's question.

She stopped on the landing and waited for me. "Probably nothing," she said with a shrug. "But you act like he's never been interested in a woman before."

"He's not interested in Mona," I said defensively.

"What planet did you just come in from?" Chris asked. "No wonder your father wanted us to leave when Porter started telling jokes. He was probably afraid he'd have to explain them all to you."

"No, he was just afraid you'd repeat one to your parents and get him in trouble," I said, feeling cranky.

We had reached the top of the stairs, and I realized we were both hesitating to go forward. It was that picture in the hallway. Neither one of us wanted to walk past it.

"Well," I said, after a moment, "should we get tough? Or should we just lie down here and sleep on the floor until my father comes up?"

"Come on," said Chris, grabbing my arm. "You wouldn't want Mona to find us here. We'll have to tough it out." She pulled me into the hallway.

If you pay attention, you'll notice that Chris always grabs my arm when she's about to act brave.

We started out at a pretty good pace, but slowed down as soon as we got near that group of pictures. Stupid, now that I stop to think about it. The smart thing would have been to put our heads down and run like crazy. All we accomplished by inching along that way was to torture ourselves. We probably looked like total idiots, moving in slow motion, holding each other's hands, and watching those pictures as though one of them was going to jump off the wall and attack us.

When neither of us saw or felt a thing, I didn't know whether to be relieved or disappointed.

Later that night, when I woke up and saw the ghost standing at the foot of my bed, I realized I had been both relieved and disappointed. Now, however, I was just plain terrified.

CHAPTER NINE

A Southern Gentleman

If ghosts could talk it would be a lot easier to figure out what they want. Actually, maybe they can. But you'd never know it from the two I've met so far.

Anyway, it would have simplified things if I could have just said, "What are you doing here?" and gotten some kind of answer. Probably I should have tried. But the truth is, I don't think I could have managed it. The way he stood there, just looking beautiful and staring at us with those terrible dark eyes, made it hard to think about talking.

I lay there for a while, trembling under my blankets and listening to Chris snore, which was something I hadn't known about her before. I was trying to figure out what to do. Should I say something to the ghost? Should I try to wake Chris? Or should I just scream, and hope that he would do a quick fade?

I wasn't sure whether or not the ghost knew I was awake. That was mostly because I had woken up slowly. If I hadn't, I probably would have let out a scream that would have roused everyone in the inn. I may have gotten used to spotting spooks by this time, but I still wasn't used to waking up and finding one in my bedroom.

The ghost had a puzzled look on his face. I wondered if he was trying to figure out why I had been able to see him. It had obviously been a big surprise.

I don't have a real answer to that question, by the way. My theory is that after our experience with the Woman in White Chris and I had become sensitized to ghosts, and could see them more easily than most people.

I finally decided to try to wake Snoring Beauty—mostly because I figured she would kill me if she found out I had let her sleep through a ghostly appearance. And she'd have to find out, because I was going to need someone to talk this over with in the morning.

The problem was, how to wake her up without scaring off the ghost. I didn't want to spook the spook, if you know what I mean.

That sounds a little backward, doesn't it? After all, people are supposed to be frightened of ghosts, not the other way around. But I was starting to feel a little more comfortable with this one. I still wasn't convinced that he was harmless. But at the moment I had the feeling he had come visiting mostly out of curiosity. And if he *was* dangerous, I figured I would just as soon have Chris awake to help me out.

I considered doing a little snoring myself. If it was loud enough, it might wake her. But I decided the ghost would know I was faking, and might not be amused. Finally I gave up trying to be fancy and just called her name. Either it would work or it wouldn't. Keeping my eyes on the ghost, I whispered "Chris. Oh, Chris! I've got a little surprise for you!"

Snorts and sputters from the other bed. (She's going to kill me when she reads this. But it's true.)

"Oh, Chris. We've got company."

Snort, snort. Sputter, sputter.

"He's beautiful, and you can see right through him."

I swear, if you're talking about men Chris will hear you even in her sleep. Her eyes popped open. Then she let out the kind of yelp I'd managed to avoid so far.

The ghost shimmered and almost disappeared. His shape got all wobbly for a minute. I held my breath, hoping Chris would have the good sense to be quiet.

She did, and the two of us lay there as if we had been frozen. Finally the ghost came back into focus.

Unfortunately, my father chose that moment to pound on the door.

The ghost looked startled. An instant later he was gone. But before he faded out of sight, he took a moment to do something wonderful. Sweeping off his hat, he made a deep bow. Then he put his fingers to his lips—and blew us a kiss.

Chris clapped her hands over her heart. "I think I'm in love," she whispered.

My father rapped on the door again. "Nine. Chris. Are you in there?" He sounded worried.

I got out of bed and slipped on my bathrobe. "What's up?" I asked, opening the door.

He didn't just sound worried. He looked worried. And a little confused.

"Well, I'm glad you two are safe and sound," he said.

"Shouldn't we be?" I asked, ignoring the fact that we had just been visited by a ghost.

"Of course you should," he said. "But there's something strange going on. Were you two in my room tonight?"

"Not since before supper," I said.

"Well, there goes one theory," he muttered.

"What's going on?" I asked.

"Come here," he said, making a gesture with his head. "You, too, Chris."

Chris scrambled out of bed and grabbed her robe. The two of us followed him out of our room and into the hallway. Mona was standing near the door of his room, looking puzzled. I was not amused. Dad gestured toward the door of his room, and I peeked inside.

It was a mess. The dresser drawers were half-open. Clothes were scattered all over the floor. The mattress had been pushed sideways so it was almost falling off the bed.

"What happened?" I asked.

"I don't know," he said. "Mona and I got into a discussion about the inn, and I was going to show her some of the preliminary sketches I had made today. When we got up here, I found this."

"Was anything stolen?" asked Chris.

"Only one thing," said my father, looking puzzled. "The original floor plans Baltimore gave me this afternoon."

CHAPTER TEN

Mona Makes Her Move

"Well, I'd say the butler did it," said Chris, spitting a mouthful of toothpaste into the sink. "Except the place doesn't have one."

We were standing in the bathroom—the one we shared with six other rooms—getting ready for breakfast. It was fairly late in the morning, since we hadn't had the kind of night that leaves one feeling rested. After the episode with the ghost, we had spent another half hour with my father, who grilled us on whether or not we had heard anything suspicious. Since the ghost hadn't made a sound, we could honestly tell him that we hadn't. When the questioning didn't get him anywhere, he just sat down in the hallway and stared at the opposite wall. "I don't get it," he said. "I just don't get it."

Mona slid down beside him and patted his shoulder. "I'm sure they'll turn up, Henry," she said gently.

I had thought about telling her his name was *Mr.* Tanleven, but decided it wasn't a good idea.

I took my toothbrush out of my mouth. "Well, I wouldn't guess the butler, anyway," I said. "I think it was Mona."

Chris wiped a smear of toothpaste off her face. "You sound like you're jealous," she said.

"Could be," I replied. "But if you'll remember, it was Mona who left the parlor for about fifteen minutes last night."

"So she had to freshen her makeup," said Chris. "Women do that. Meg Coleman was out of the room when we got there. Why don't you suspect her?"

"That sweet little old lady? She's not the type."

Chris laughed out loud. "Now I know you're not thinking like a detective. The ones who aren't the type are usually the ones who did it. Besides, if Mona already had the plans, why would she have come up with your father to look at them?"

"To throw suspicion somewhere else," I said. "She probably figured if she was there when the crime was discovered, people wouldn't even begin to suspect her."

"And what's her motive?" asked Chris.

"I don't know. What's anyone's motive? That's the biggest mystery of all right now. What does someone have to gain by stealing those plans?"

"Well, I still think you're jumping to conclusions about Mona," said Chris. "I bet everyone at that party left the room long enough to have stolen the plans at some point or another.

And that's not counting Dieter, or Martha and Isabella, or even Peter."

"Peter doesn't live here," I pointed out.

"No, but I'll bet he has a key. He's probably in and out all the time. No one would even think twice if they saw him."

"You think Peter did it?" I asked, stepping back out into the hallway.

"Don't be dense. I'm just saying it's too early to start narrowing down the list of suspects. I'd say the only people we can count out right now are you, me, and your father. And if we didn't know him so well, we'd have to leave him in, too."

I looked at her.

"Well, it could be one of those crazy self-destructive plots," she said. "They have them on TV all the time."

"That's why TV rots your brain," I replied. "What about Baltimore? Can't we cross him off the list? After all, he does own the place."

Chris shook her head. "He's definitely still a suspect. For the same reason."

"You can't be serious," I said.

She shrugged. "Who knows what kind of plot might be going on here? Until we can figure out a logical reason why someone would want those plans, we have to keep all the possibilities open."

We had been walking down the hall as we talked and had reached the set of old pictures. "Do you think *he* has anything to do with it?" I asked, indicating the photograph of the long-dead Confederate soldier who had stood in our room the night before.

Chris shrugged. "Doesn't seem likely," she said. "For one thing, ghosts don't seem to move things around much."

I nodded.

"Besides, he's just too gorgeous."

I laughed. "Now who's not thinking like a detective?" I asked. But as I stared at the picture, I knew what Chris meant.

"Ah," said a voice behind us. "I see you're admiring the ghost of the Quackadoodle Inn!"

I turned and saw Porter Markson standing behind us. His hands were tucked behind his back, and he smiled as he rocked back and forth on the balls of his feet.

"Didn't you know the inn is supposed to be haunted?" he asked, misinterpreting the surprised look on my face. "Well, don't let it scare you. Captain Gray has never been known to harm anyone."

"Captain Gray?" I asked.

Porter nodded. "Captain Johnny Gray. Legend has it he was the most handsome man in Charleston, South Carolina."

"Well, what's he doing haunting an inn here in New York State?" asked Chris.

Porter shrugged. "Who knows? To tell you the truth, I've never actually seen him. Sometimes I think the whole legend was cooked up by one of the previous owners just to get people interested in the inn."

I decided not to tell him how wrong he was about that!

"Are you ladies heading down to breakfast?" he asked.

"Yes!" said Chris emphatically. "I'm starving!"

That was no surprise. Hunger is sort of a permanent condition with Chris.

"Well, if you don't mind some company, I'll come with you."

That was fine with us. I figured we could pump him for more information about the ghost while we ate.

Breakfast turned out to be coffee and pastries, set out in the dining room for anyone who wanted them. They called this a Continental Breakfast. That means it's European. For some reason sophisticated people call Europe *The* Continent—as if the other six didn't exist! It sounds stuck-up to me, but that's the way it is. Chris happily poured herself a cup of coffee from the big silver urn. I made a face and went looking for some milk. I don't know how she can drink that stuff!

When the three of us finally settled down to start stuffing Dieter's glorious pastries into our mouths, it struck me that we were the only ones in the dining room.

"Where's everyone else?" I asked.

Porter blew across the top of his coffee. "Well, probably people have either eaten or decided to sleep late. Dieter leaves breakfast out until eleven o'clock." He leaned forward and lowered his voice. "Of course, there are *only* seven guests anyway."

"I wonder why?" asked Chris.

Porter shrugged. "The inn's not doing very well. Things will pick up a little this weekend. It's Thursday, so probably a few people will show up today. There might be a fairly good crowd come Friday. And, of course, there's the dance on Saturday. That should draw some extra guests."

"Why isn't the inn doing well?" I asked, thinking Porter might know something useful.

Before he could answer, Mona Curtis came sailing into the room. "Oh, there you are, Nine," she said. "I was just looking for you! Could you come and talk to me a minute?"

"Good grief!" whispered Chris. "Do you suppose she proposed to your father already?"

I glared at Chris, then tried to get my face back under control before I went to talk to Mona. I don't think I quite managed it, because when I got to her table the first thing she said was, "For heaven's sakes, don't look so apprehensive. This is a business talk. It has nothing to do with your father."

Before I could decide how to answer that comment, she asked me to wait while she got some coffee. I watched unhappily as she crossed the room; little as I liked to admit it, Mona was a very attractive woman. That morning she was wearing a peach and yellow cotton sweater. I had seen one something like it in a magazine a few weeks before. Very expensive! Her dark hair brushed across her face as she bent to examine the pastry tray. Her long fingers hovered over the goodies before reaching out to pluck up a cheese danish. My mind changed the image to a vision of a giant Mona, reaching out to snatch up my father.

I began pressing my fingertips against the white linen tablecloth, to see how red I could get them. That may sound stupid, but it gave me something to think about.

"I can't have a serious conversation without my morning coffee," said Mona, slipping back into her chair. She poured some cream into her steaming cup and stirred it. I wondered if she would realize I was faking if I sneezed and knocked the coffee into her lap.

She tapped her spoon against the edge of her cup a couple of times and then set it down. It was the closest thing I had seen to a nervous gesture on her part.

"Well, let's get right down to business," she said.

"OK," I answered. I was dying to know what this was all about.

Mona smiled. *Vulture,* I thought.

Then she struck. "I was wondering," she said, stirring her coffee again, "if you might like to write a book for me."

I fell off my chair.

CHAPTER ELEVEN

The Deadly Wildflower Bandits

I heard Chris snort when I hit the floor. It would have made me angry, except I knew I probably would have done the same thing. Porter jumped to his feet, but sat back down again when he saw that I wasn't hurt. Mona just raised one eyebrow. "Are you all right?" she asked after I had climbed back into my chair.

"Fine," I said. "Only I think my ears have gone bad. I thought I heard you ask if I wanted to write a book."

Mona nodded. "Your ears are fine," she said. "Your father told me you had a very interesting experience with a ghost earlier this summer. He also told me you kept a journal about it. I asked him to let me read a few pages. I think it's pretty good."

Now this was a complicated situation! The idea that my father had shown this woman the journal I had let him take made me angry. But how angry could I really get, when the result was so interesting?

Mona stirred her coffee. "I'm not making any promises," she said. "But the fact is, I edit kids' books for a living, and your adventure in the Grand Theater sounds interesting. If you'd be willing to let me read the rest of the journal, I'll give it serious consideration. If I think it can work, I'll tell you what you would have to do to turn it into a book."

"I need time to think," I said, sliding out of my seat.

Mona shrugged. "No hurry," she said. "I'll be here through Sunday."

"Well," said Chris, when I got back to the table, "what was *that* all about?"

"I'll tell you later," I said.

I was a little nervous, because in the time it had taken me to walk back to my table, I had realized I wasn't sure how Chris was going to react to this news. I mean, if it were the other way around, I would have had two feelings. I'd be glad for Chris, of course. After all, she *is* my best friend. But I'd also be so jealous I'd probably explode.

I wished I could figure out a way to discuss Mona's offer with my father before I had to explain it to Chris. But she was sitting right there, and she wasn't about to let me get away without telling her what the woman had wanted. I wouldn't have, either, if it had been the other way around.

Porter Markson slid away from the table. "I guess I'd better get moving," he said. "I'm going for a little hike today. I'll see you girls at dinner."

"OK, Nine," said Chris when Porter had left the dining room. "*Now* will you tell me what this is all about?"

"Let's go outside," I said.

We went to stand on the little bridge that crossed the stream. I told Chris what Mona had offered to do.

"That's great!" she said.

Then she got real quiet.

I tapped a finger on the side of her head. "Yoo-hoo. Anybody home?"

"Why didn't you tell me you were keeping a diary?" she asked. She sounded hurt.

"What was to tell?" I said and threw a twig into the water. I watched the stream carry it away from us.

"I was just keeping a record of what we did while we solved that mystery. My father asked if he could read some of it, and I let him. I had no idea he was going to show it to some editor and tell her it might make a good book."

Chris was quiet for a moment. She tilted her head to the left, then to the right, then back again. It looked as if she had a slow motion Ping-Pong game going on in her mind. Finally she stopped, and nodded, as if she had come to some kind of decision.

She looked at me and threw her hands into the air. "I think it's wonderful!" She threw her arms around me. We started jumping up and down.

Let me tell you, it's as important to have a friend when you want to be happy as it is to have one when you're feeling lousy. But it's hard to focus on things when you're jumping up and down, so I stopped when I noticed some people coming out of the woods.

"What's wrong?" asked Chris.

"Nothing," I said. "We've just got company."

I could see now that it was Arnie and Meg Coleman. They were strolling down the path that led to the bridge, holding hands like a couple of kids. They looked sweet. I thought about my parents, and wondered why some people have to split up and others are able to stay in love all their lives.

"Howdy, youngsters!" said Arnie as he and his wife stepped on to the bridge. "Glorious morning, eh?"

I recognized that "eh." All the Canadians I've ever met tack it on to at least half their sentences.

Arnie was carrying, of all things, a shovel. And they both had buckets filled with dirt and plants.

Meg giggled. "We dug up a few wildflowers for my rock garden. I know we're not supposed to, but we didn't take anything that's endangered. You won't turn us in, will you?"

She actually seemed worried that we might be going to call the police on her.

"Your secret is safe with us," said Chris, though how she managed to keep her voice serious was beyond me.

Meg reached out a plump hand and patted Chris on the cheek. "I knew I could count on you, dear," she said with a wink. "Come on, Arnie. Let's get these back to the room before someone else catches us!"

We waited until they were out of sight. Then we broke out giggling. From that point on we referred to Arnie and Meg as The Deadly Wildflower Bandits.

We walked back to the inn to find out if there was any place nearby where we could go swimming. The lobby was empty when we entered. We could hear someone yelling in the distance. At first I thought it had to be Gloria. Then I figured it was probably Dieter.

It was a real shock when I finally figured out it was my father.

CHAPTER TWELVE

A Hole in the Wall

"Is he upset, or just excited?" asked Chris, when it dawned on her who was doing the shouting.

"I'm not sure," I said. "Let's go find out."

The sound had come from the right. We ran through the hall into the dining room. It was empty, but I could hear my father's voice more clearly now. It was coming from the kitchen. Now I realized that Deiter was yelling, too.

As we got closer to the kitchen, I could tell that Dad was happy. But Dieter was obviously very upset. I wondered what could make one of them so happy, and one of them so mad.

I didn't have to wonder long. As soon as we went through the kitchen door I could see what had upset Dieter: my father had made a mess in his kitchen. I decided right then that Dad was either braver or dumber than I had ever realized.

The little German cook was standing by the stove, waving a spoon over his head and cursing. His face was bright red. Martha and Isabella, who must have rushed in when the commotion began, stood a safe distance away from him. All three of them were looking at my father, who was standing next to a hole in the wall and wearing a big grin. The hole was about a foot wide. A pile of dusty plaster lay on the floor at Dad's feet.

"What is going on here?" asked a new voice.

It was Baltimore who had just come in through the back way. He had a very worried expression on his face as he surveyed the scene.

"This man—this man is *ruining* my kitchen!" cried Dieter. "There is *dust* in the air! Dust!"

"'This man' is just doing his job," said my father. "I was checking at the back side of the fireplace to make sure the wall was solid and look what I found!"

He pointed toward the hole in the wall with his flashlight. Everyone, including me, stepped forward to peek. To my surprise, I could see a tiny room inside. It was barely the size of a small closet. I could see a shelf and a small chair.

"What kind of a room is that?" asked Chris.

"I think I can answer that question," said Isabella.

Everyone turned their attention from the hole in the wall to the pretty waitress. "Well, I'm not certain," she said. "But it looks to me like the kind of room that would have been used on the Underground Railroad."

"Of course!" cried my father. "That makes perfect sense."

It may have made sense to him, but it didn't to me. I said so.

My father looked at me in astonishment. "What do they teach you in that school?" he asked.

"Well *ex-cuuu-se* me for not knowing everything!" I said.

The level of crankiness in this conversation was getting out of hand. So I was relieved when Isabella jumped in with some information.

"The Underground Railroad wasn't really a railroad," she said. "It was a system for helping escaped slaves make it north to freedom."

"Well, if they didn't go by train, how did they go?" asked Chris.

Isabella shrugged. "By foot, by mule, by boat—any way that would get them north. Sometimes they actually did travel by train, though usually that involved a lot of disguises and plotting." She smiled. "One man actually had himself nailed into a crate and shipped to Boston. But most people needed places to hide and places to find food. Those were the stops on the Underground Railroad. And the people who led the slaves north, took them from stop to stop, were called conductors."

Suddenly everything clicked into place. "You mean like Harriet Tubman?" I asked.

Isabella smiled. "That's right. Harriet Tubman is the most famous. But there were a lot of others. A very successful conductor named Samson Carter had his base of operations right around here."

"I didn't know that!" exclaimed my father. "Samson Carter is one of my heroes."

Now I didn't feel so stupid. We had read about Harriet Tubman's daring efforts to help runaway slaves last year in social studies. I had just forgotten about them for a while.

"But I don't understand why the Underground Railroad would need a stop in New York," said Chris. "This wasn't a slave state."

"That's true," said Isabella. "But a national law called the Fugitive Slave Act said runaway slaves were the property of their owners, no matter where they were. So a black could make it all the way to New York, and still get sent back to slavery. Some slave owners offered big rewards for their slaves. There was always someone willing to turn a man in for the money on his head. Runaways weren't really safe until they made it to Canada."

I shook my head. It all sounded pretty ugly. "How come you know all this stuff?" I said.

Isabella's eyes flashed. "Everyone should know it," she said. "It's part of the blood history of this country."

I thought she was going to pick up where my father had left off, and finish the lecture on being undereducated. But the moment passed. "Anyway," she said softly, "I suppose I'm more interested than most people would be, since I come from slave blood myself."

I looked at her in surprise.

"I'm one quarter black," she said. "That makes me what they used to call a quadroon—

plenty black enough to have been a slave myself."

I swallowed uneasily.

Chris took over. "If there were rewards, why would the people who owned this place have helped runaways hide here?" she asked.

"Because some people think what's right is more important than what's profitable," said Isabella. "More important than what's comfortable, too, since it was illegal to hide a runaway slave. Anyone who did it, black *or* white, was risking trouble with the law. They could face the kind of fines that would bankrupt them, or even be thrown in jail. But that didn't stop people who believed in freedom. They helped the runaways in spite of the law."

I walked over to the hole my father had made and peered into the little room. It was about two feet wide and three feet long. I thought about the people who might have hidden there, the black women and men risking their lives to get to Canada so they could be free.

I thought about being closed up in there, in the dark. It was such a small space! I wondered how long people had to stay in there. I didn't think I could have done it.

"Why was it sealed up like that?" asked Chris, who had come over to stand beside me.

This time my father answered. "Since it was used as a place for people to hide, I would guess that the door itself was disguised, somehow made to blend in with the rest of the wall. Probably years after the room was last used, some-

one covered the door without even knowing it
was here." He turned to Baltimore. "I'd suggest
that we restore the space to its original condition. It will make the Quackadoodle a little
more special, give people something to tell their
friends about after they've stayed here."

Isabella's eyes flashed, and she started to
say something. My father cut her off.

"Yes, I know. That sounds 'commercial.' But
it works two ways. At the same time that it
brings in extra customers for Baltimore, it
teaches people about something you think is
pretty important."

"I do not care important!" cried Dieter. "I
care my kitchen! I don't want people tramping
through here to look in a little hole while I am
trying to cook!"

"Maybe we should talk about this later," my
father said to Baltimore.

The innkeeper nodded.

Dieter figured Dad was just trying to get
around him and started to yell again.

I was trying to think of some way to keep
everyone happy when I felt Chris grab my elbow.
I turned and saw that she was looking through
the hole. She yanked on my arm, indicating I
should come and look, too. Something about the
way she was standing, the way she held my
elbow, let me know this was important.

I glanced around. The grown-ups were busy
yelling at one another, so I squeezed up against
Chris and peered into the opening.

The ghost was sitting there, looking back.

CHAPTER THIRTEEN

And With a Crook of His Finger, He Beckoned Us On

Between the argument behind us and the ghost in front of us, I was finding it hard to think. I was sure he wanted something from us, but I didn't know what.

Finally I just decided to ask. "What do you want?" I whispered.

I didn't really think he could answer me. It was just that I didn't know what else to do.

To my surprise, Captain Gray stood up and pointed to the wall in front of him. But before I could see what he was pointing at, I heard Baltimore shout, "Watch out!"

An instant later I heard a loud crash.

I spun around in time to see the next plate go flying through the air. It hit the wall and spattered into hundreds of pieces. Another one followed it, and then another.

"You want a messy kitchen?" cried Dieter. "I'll show you a messy kitchen!" He grabbed a fifth plate and flung it across the room. He didn't seem to be throwing them at anyone in particular. Even so, I was a little worried about what might happen if he ran out of plates and started on the knives.

Chris was feeling the same way. "Come on," she said. "It's time to beat feet."

"But the ghost—"

"He's gone," said Chris. "He took off when the fireworks started."

"But I can't leave my father with this maniac!"

"Your father's the one who started this. He ought to know better than to poke holes in crazy people's walls!"

I was about to answer when Gloria walked into the room. She took one look at what was going on, and put an end to it.

"Dieter, stop acting so silly."

That was all she said. But her tone of voice probably would have brought a rampaging rhinoceros to a halt. Dieter stopped. I wasn't surprised.

She turned to Baltimore. "Why do you let him do that?" she asked.

Before he could answer, she turned and waved her hands at the rest of us. "Everybody out of here!" she said. "This man has work to do."

Chris was right. It was time to beat feet.

Without saying a word, we headed for the little bridge. It had become our place to talk, much like the oak tree in the cemetery at home.

"Well, the ghost wants something from us," said Chris, once we had settled ourselves against the railing. "That much is clear."

I nodded. The question was, what did he want? "There are too many things that don't make sense here," I said. "To begin with, why is an inn in New York State haunted by a ghost from South Carolina?"

Chris nodded. "And does the fact that this place used to be a stop on the Underground Railroad have anything to do with the ghost? I can't see how they are connected. But they have to be, somehow."

"That's the problem with ghosts," I said. "You can't just figure out what's going on. You've got to figure out what *went* on."

"Speaking of goings on, what about the original plans for the inn? The ones stolen from your father's room? Do they fit into all this, or is that part of something else altogether?"

This was getting to be too much. I sat on the edge of the bridge and took off my shoes so I could dangle my toes in the water. I thought for a minute, then said, "As far as I'm concerned, the only person around here who's not a suspect is the ghost."

Even that changed as the day went on. Not that we began to suspect the ghost of stealing the plans. But we ended up with more non-suspects. As Porter had predicted, several new people checked into the inn before evening.

Watching them come in, Chris and I decided we were glad the theft had happened on Wednesday, when there were fewer people around. It kept the possibilities down to a reasonable number.

The problem was, we couldn't figure out how to narrow the suspects down any further. By dinner we were as far from figuring things out as we had been when the day began.

Our second dinner at the Quackadoodle was very different from our first. In addition to the new people registered at the inn, others had come just for dinner, and the dining room was nearly half-full. That meant Baltimore and Gloria were tied up with the customers. Also, Arnie and Meg Coleman chose to sit by themselves that night.

That left only five of us from the previous night's party. Of course, Dad, Chris, and I could have eaten by ourselves, like the Colemans. But my father had already asked Mona if she would like to join us. Then Porter Markson wandered into the dining room, and we decided to ask him if he would like to sit with us, too.

I figured Chris and I should enjoy the company while we could. In another day or so my father would probably be asking us to eat by ourselves, so he could have a private dinner with Mona.

I was not amused by the idea.

Actually, I was very confused. I mean, there I was, peacefully feeling cranky and nasty toward Mona, when she went and offered to do this wonderful thing of helping me turn my diary into a book. Now I wasn't sure how I should feel about her.

I was trying to sort that out when I heard her ask my father about the little room he had found earlier in the day.

"To tell you the truth, it wasn't entirely accidental," Dad said. He sounded a trifle smug. "When I went over the plans before they were stolen, I noticed that they didn't quite match the actual construction of the inn. So I thought there might be something there—although I wasn't expecting what I actually found."

"What about the plans?" asked Porter. "Is anything being done about getting them back?"

Dad shrugged. "Baltimore said that as long as nothing of mine had been stolen, he would prefer not to call the police. He's afraid it would be bad publicity for the inn. I had mixed feelings about that. But by the time he was done describing how incompetent the local law was, I agreed to go along with him. They *were* his plans after all."

Porter nodded. "I think Baltimore's right. He's having enough trouble getting people here now."

That got the grown-ups into a discussion of public relations, which became very boring very fast. Chris and I excused ourselves. Normally my father might have asked me to stay at the table for a while. But with Mona there, he was perfectly willing to let me go.

I didn't really like leaving him alone with her, but Chris and I had made plans for the evening. The fact that we had Mona to keep my father out of our hair made things a lot easier.

"What time shall I set the alarm for?" I asked, when we got back to our room.

Chris thought for a moment. "Two o'clock," she said. "By then even the night owls should be sound asleep."

"Two o'clock it is," I said, pulling out the little plunger on the back of the clock. I glanced at the face. It was quarter of eight. "I haven't been to sleep this early in years," I said.

"Neither have I," said Chris. "But then, it's been a long time since I got as little sleep as I did last night. And tonight's not going to be any better. So let's get some rest now. We'll need it if we're going to sneak back into the kitchen and figure out what Captain Gray wanted us to see."

I nodded.

It seemed like only minutes later when the alarm went off. I opened my eyes and let out a little gasp. With that quick waking I hadn't had time to prepare myself for the sight of the ghost standing at the foot of my bed.

This time I didn't hesitate. "Chris!" I hissed. "Chris, wake up. He's here again."

She sputtered a bit, and then lifted her head and began rubbing her eyes.

The ghost didn't even waver. I figured he must be getting used to us.

For a moment no one said anything. The two of us lay in our beds, looking at the ghost. He stood there looking back.

Finally I couldn't stand it anymore. "What do you want?" I asked.

He smiled. (That ghost had *the* most gorgeous smile!) Then he crooked one finger and made a gesture that indicated he wanted us to follow him.

Then he walked through the door.

"Quick!" yelled Chris. "Grab your flashlight."

I jumped out of bed and stifled a yelp. The floor was cold on my bare feet. I started scrabbling under my bed for my slippers.

"We don't have time for that!" said Chris impatiently. "Let's get moving!"

Unlike Captain Gray, we had to open the door. When we tumbled into the hall, he was waiting for us.

He nodded and then started walking down the hallway in that strange, floating kind of way that ghosts have.

I looked at Chris. She looked at me.

We began to follow him.

CHAPTER FOURTEEN

The Attic

I had expected Captain Gray to lead us back to the kitchen. But when he reached the stairwell, he went up, instead of down.

Suddenly this expedition didn't seem like such a good idea. It was one thing to go back to the familiar territory of the first floor. Going up to the third floor, which we hadn't even seen, seemed far more frightening. I didn't know what we were apt to find up there.

I stood at the foot of the stairs, not moving. That was a mistake, since the only move that would get me out of that situation was a swift step backward. I didn't figure that out soon enough, which gave Chris, who does not believe in hesitating, time to grab my elbow. "Come on," she said as she began dragging me up the stairs after Captain Gray.

When I complained about that later, her response was: "You stand around and think and think, and then decide to do whatever it is, anyway. Why should we waste all that time, when we can just go ahead and *do* it?"

79

So there we were, two eleven-year-old girls, dressed in nightgowns and carrying nothing but one flashlight, following a ghost up the stairs of a creepy old inn. When I write about it now, I don't know how I managed to keep from turning around and running back to my room. I guess it was mostly because of Chris; one thing I've learned from all this ghost stuff is that nothing is quite as scary when you share it with a friend. Besides, I wasn't about to admit that I was too scared to follow her someplace that she was willing to lead. (Please notice, though, the way she grabbed my arm before she started.)

We tiptoed slowly up the stairs, trying not to make a sound. If we woke anyone, I didn't think we could count on the ghost to hang around and prove our story. We'd sound like a couple of idiots. We'd also get in a lot of trouble.

When we reached the third floor, I aimed the flashlight down the hallway. It appeared much the same as the second floor, except that there weren't any pictures on the walls. The ghost continued gliding down the hall. We had to scurry to keep up with him. Scurrying isn't easy when you're trying not to make any noise.

At the end of the hallway the ghost faded through another door. Chris and I stopped. The idea of opening that door seemed scarier than anything we had done so far that night.

For a moment I thought we might turn back.

I should have known better.

"Well, here goes nothing," Chris whispered. She put out her hand and turned the knob.

The door swung open with a creak.

On the other side, by the light of the flashlight, we could see a long, dark stairway. The ghost was standing at the top of the stairs, looking down at us.

"M-m-must be the attic," I stammered. I wasn't too pleased. I have a thing about attics. I think an attic is the scariest place in anyone's house.

As I had expected, the ghost wanted us to follow him. When he beckoned, Chris grabbed my arm and started up the bare wooden steps. They were very cold, compared to the carpeting we had been walking on. The flashlight wobbled in my trembling hand. I wondered what we were getting ourselves into.

The attic ceiling was low, only a foot or two above our heads. A tall man would have had to duck to walk there. The roof was supported by broad beams. It had never been insulated, and we could see the actual wood of the roof.

I pointed the flashlight in different directions. The place looked like a giant yard sale. Generations worth of stuff that was broken, worn-out, or just plain out of style was piled wherever we looked.

The ghost was standing at one end of the attic, waiting for us.

"Come on," said Chris again. "I think he's getting impatient."

"Or tired," I said.

I have a theory that it's fairly hard work for ghosts to show themselves. Of course, Chris and I seemed to be able to see Captain Gray when no one else could. But if he wanted to be *sure* we saw him, I figured he was *working* at being visible.

The attic floor was even colder than the stairs had been. I wished I had taken the time to put on my slippers.

Moving toward the ghost, we walked past broken chairs, boxes of old dishes, battered suitcases, and piles of lumpy mattresses. Nervous as I was, I really wanted to stop and open some of the more interesting looking boxes.

The ghost was standing next to a large, badly battered trunk. It was made of wood and had a rounded top. The brass latches were undone.

The ghost looked at the trunk and nodded.

Obviously, we were supposed to open it.

I wasn't particularly thrilled by the idea. For some reason, I expected it to be like one of those trick peanut-brittle cans—you know, the kind where you take off the top and all these fake snakes come flying out.

I think something like that must have occurred to Chris, too. "Here, I'll hold the flashlight while you open it," she said.

"You have *got* to be kidding!"

"Shhh!" she whispered. "Let's not argue in front of the ghost!"

I glanced over at Captain Gray. He was starting to look kind of cranky.

I set the flashlight on a nearby chair, so that its beam fell on the trunk.

"Here," I said. "You take one side, I'll take the other."

Chris nodded. We knelt at opposite sides of the trunk.

"Ready? she asked.

"Ready," I whispered.

We lifted the lid.

CHAPTER FIFTEEN

The Trunk

Nothing jumped out of the trunk. What did happen was that as soon as we had the lid up, the ghost disappeared. It was as if someone had turned off a light. *Click.* One second he was there, the next he was gone.

"My goodness, Toto," I said, "People come and go in the strangest way around here."

"Come back from Oz and let's get down to business," replied Chris. "I figure if Captain Gray went to all that work to get us up here, there must be something pretty important in this trunk. So let's find it."

I got the flashlight and pointed its beam into the trunk.

"I don't get it," said Chris.

I didn't either. I was expecting something from Civil War times. All I saw was a stack of clothes that looked like things I had seen in pictures of my parents when they were hippy teenagers: paisley shirts, bell-bottom trousers, and fringed vests—things like that.

"Maybe there's something else underneath that stuff," I said.

We started digging. Ten minutes later we had emptied the trunk. We were surrounded by stacks of old clothes, a complete run of *Popular Mechanics* from 1963 to 1966, a broken waffle iron, a toothless comb, and fifteen record albums by three groups I had never heard of. With the possible exception of the comb, none of it looked like it was any older than my father.

"What does any of this have to do with Captain Gray?" Chris asked.

"You've got me," I said, shining the flashlight into the empty trunk. Something about the way it looked bothered me. Unfortunately, I couldn't figure out what it was.

I looked at the stack of clothes again.

"Pockets!" I cried.

"Shhh!" hissed Chris. "You'll wake someone up."

"Let's check the pockets," I said, pointing to the clothes. "Maybe there's something in there."

"I bet you're right!" she whispered.

Ten minutes later we had been through all the clothing. The only thing we had to show for our efforts was a handful of buttons. Two said "Peace," one said "Frodo Lives!" and three more had words I didn't know you were allowed to wear in public.

I looked at the empty trunk. I looked at the mess we had made. I felt we had let the ghost down.

It made me sad.

"Come on," Chris said. "We'd better pack this thing up and get out of here. We can figure out what to do next over breakfast."

Slowly we folded the clothes and put them back into the trunk.

We were halfway down the attic stairs before I finally realized what it was that had bothered me about the trunk. Chris had given me the clue when she had asked if we should go back to our original plan and make our way down to the kitchen to check out the little room.

Suddenly everything clicked into place. "I think I've got it!" I said. Grabbing Chris by the arm, I turned and headed back up the stairs.

"What are you doing?" she asked.

"Wait and see." I didn't want to tell her, because I figured I would look really stupid if I was wrong. By the time I had finished dumping everything out of the trunk again, I realized I was going to look stupid if I was wrong, whether I said anything or not.

I knelt in front of the empty trunk and put one arm inside it until my hand was resting on the bottom. Then I put my other hand on the floor.

"I knew it!" I cried in triumph.

"What are you doing?" asked Chris again.

I told her to do what I had just done. Looking skeptical, she knelt and repeated my actions. A look of understanding crossed her face as she leaned on one arm, and then the other. When you did that it was easy to tell that the hand in the trunk was almost two inches higher than the hand on the floor.

"A false bottom," she said. "How did you figure it out?"

I shrugged. "It just didn't look right to me. But I couldn't figure out why. When you mentioned the hidden room downstairs, I realized it was the same kind of thing: the inside and the outside didn't quite match."

"That's terrific," said Chris. "But how do we get into it?"

It was forty-five minutes before we answered that question. In that time we poked, prodded, and pried at that trunk in every way we could think of. We turned it upside down and sideways looking for buttons to press or panels to pull. We shook it. We pressed every one of the brass studs. Nothing happened, until Chris finally slapped the side of the trunk in anger and said, "This is impossible!"

I was the one who heard the click. Looking into the trunk, I saw that the bottom had tilted up just slightly. I reached in and pressed on the back of it. The front came up more. I pressed a little harder. A gap appeared between the bottom and the trunk wall closest to us. I slipped in my finger and pulled up. It was like opening a door.

"Nice work!" whispered Chris, who had been holding the flashlight.

We bent over the trunk and looked in.

The secret compartment was about an inch and a half deep. It held only two things: a book and a red stone the size of a small grape.

Chris took the stone out of the compartment and set it in the palm of her hand. I pointed the flashlight at it. It sparkled in the light, which seemed to penetrate right to its center.

She looked at me in astonishment. "I think this thing is a ruby!"

CHAPTER SIXTEEN

The Diary

Chris and I sat side by side on my bed. The ruby was hidden in the bottom drawer of our dresser. As excited as we were about finding it, for the time being the book had all our attention.

It was about an inch thick and bound in brown leather. The cover was blank. But when we opened it and saw the words, "The Diary of Captain Jonathan Gray" written on the first page, I felt a tingle skitter down my spine.

I looked at Chris. "Now we're getting somewhere," she whispered. I nodded my head—and turned the page.

I could *tell* you about what we read there. But I think it's time to let Captain Gray speak for himself. So the rest of this chapter is in his words, just as we found them in his diary.

APRIL 21, 1863

Today I was given a great responsibility. Some of the finest women of Charleston, knowing of our desperate need for weapons and supplies, have volunteered their gold and their jewelry for the good of the Confederate cause.

The things we need can best be purchased in Canada. But the Canadians will not accept our currency. So it is necessary for someone to carry the actual treasure to Canada.

I have been asked to do the job because of the years I spent at college in Massachusetts, which left me with the ability to imitate the way a Yankee speaks. It's a skill I will need if I am to pass safely through Yankee territory.

It is such a great honor to be entrusted with this treasure, which was wrung from the very hearts of the fairest women in Charleston. I hope that I will be worthy of it.

I leave in the morning. I am to make contact with a Canadian courier in New York State three weeks from today. It will be a perilous journey. But I have a list of contacts in Maryland, Pennsylvania, and New York—friends sympathetic to the Confederate cause. They will shelter me and help speed me on my mission. It seems ironic that I will be traveling in much the same way as those slaves who escaped to the North on the infamous Underground Railroad.

APRIL 28, 1863

The journey is taking longer than I expected. The effects of the war can be seen everywhere—in the scorched fields and the burned houses, and most of all in the haunted, weary eyes of the women and

children who have lived too close to battle for too
long.

I begin to wonder if it is really worth it.

APRIL 30, 1863

Yesterday I entered Maryland. Tomorrow a
friend will take me by wagon to a train station. The
next leg of my journey will be by a real railroad,
rather than this "underground railroad" I have been
using.

This friend also offered me the use of his own
trunk, which has a cleverly constructed false bottom.
I can use this to hide the jewels, and travel with less
fear of being robbed.

MAY 9, 1863

I reached New York a day and a half ago. Canada seems within striking distance! I am staying at
a small inn called the Quackadoodle, where I am to
wait for my Canadian contact. He should be here in
three days.

I have seen a great number of blacks since I entered the state. I cannot help but believe that many
of them are escaped slaves. How it angers me to see
the property of good Southern gentlemen being sheltered by these Northerners. It is theft, pure and simple.

MAY 15, 1863

I have been here six days now, and my contact
has not yet appeared. I begin to wonder if something
has happened to him.

It would not bother me quite so much, save that
another guest here at the inn has taken an unusual
interest in me. I suspect he has noticed the occa-
sional touch of Dixie in my speech, and wonders why
I am here, what I am up to.

MAY 17, 1863

Last night, while I was at dinner, someone
searched my room. Thanks to the secret compartment in my friend's trunk, they did not find the treasure. I also keep this journal in that compartment,
so that no one can learn of it by reading these pages.

Despite the thief's failure, I am not sure that
another attempt would not succeed. What if, in frustration, the thief simply smashed the trunk? I may
be worrying needlessly. But I think I should hide the
jewels elsewhere.

MAY 31, 1863

It has been two weeks since I have written a
word in this journal. The reason is simple: I have
been unconscious that long.

On Tuesday night I buried the treasure in a se-
cluded spot. It was good fortune that I took this action, for later that same evening my unknown
enemy attacked me in my room.

I suspect that someone has betrayed me. Although I have let slip no word of my mission, after I was knocked unconscious, my assailant ransacked my room. I wonder now if someone has trailed me all the way from South Carolina, waiting for the right moment to steal the fortune they knew I was carrying. Or perhaps someone who was aware of my mission wrote ahead to unscrupulous allies to tell them what they might find in my room.

The kind of people I am dealing with is indicated by the fact that, finding nothing in the room to steal, they left me for dead.

I am alive today entirely due to the kindness of two men: the innkeeper, who discovered me, and a black man whom he called in to treat me. The latter is a remarkable person, and I will write more of him tomorrow. I must stop now, for even this little exertion has exhausted me.

JUNE 1, 1863

According to the innkeeper, my "doctor" is named Sam. He either doesn't know, or isn't willing, to give me his last name.

The strange thing is, I feel as if I have seen the man before. I find I am eager for him to arrive today, partly because I know that I am still very ill, and partly because he seems to carry with him a kind of calm, as if he had some personal source of peace and happiness. I find it a remarkable thing.

JUNE 5, 1863

Bad news. I lost consciousness after writing the last entry, and I have been asleep for another three days. According to the innkeeper, Sam was beside me almost night and day.

For the first time I fear that I might not recover. I seem to see the shadow of death hanging over me.

I worry, too, that my Canadian contact may have come and gone while I was unconscious.

JUNE 6, 1863

What a strange situation this is! I have finally recognized my doctor. He is none other than Samson Carter, so well known for his work on the Underground Railroad. What strange fate has put my life in the hands of this man?

I called him by name. He looked surprised, and even a little frightened. And no wonder. At one time there was a reward of $10,000 on his head, available to anyone who could catch him and carry him to the authorities of any slave state. That was why he looked familiar to me, of course. I had seen his face on wanted posters throughout the South.

I am in a great deal of pain now, and it is hard to sleep. Carter sat with me through the day and well into the night. To pass the time, he told me stories of his adventures with the Underground Railroad. I am impressed by the man's bravery. I know many white men who would not risk half so much for their own freedom as he has risked for people not known to him.

JUNE 7, 1863

Weak and exhausted. Two men came looking for me today—claimed they had heard there was a rebel officer being sheltered here.

Carter took me down to the kitchen, where he hid me in a little room that he told me was once used by the Underground Railroad.

"This wasn't made for white men," he said. "Least, not any that had slaves. But I guess it don't matter now. The important thing is to keep you from being skinned alive, Cap'n Gray."

I looked at him in astonishment. "How do you know who I am?" I asked.

"Oh, I knew a lot of white folk around Charleston," said Carter. "Did a lot of work down there when I was younger."

"Why didn't you turn me in when you first saw me?" I asked.

Carter shrugged. "I didn't know why you was here. Maybe you was running away, just like so many of my folk. Maybe not. I don't turn people in till I know what they're about. Now, you just rest quiet till we get the mess out front settled down."

Then he closed the door on me. I was all alone in the tiny room. It was completely black. I was ill. I could hardly hold myself up. But I feared that if I fell it would make a noise that would attract the attention of the searchers.

I thought of the stories Carter had told me, while sitting by my bed, and wondered how many frightened, sick blacks had huddled in this same hole, fearing for their lives, fearing they would be discovered.

When Carter finally came to get me, I was shivering with fever.

DATE UNKNOWN; *I have lost track of time.*

I have been lost in strange dreams. I have seen myself as a slave, in chains, beaten, placed on the block and sold. I cry out, but do not seem to be able to wake.

Carter is here. When I rouse myself I see him. Sometimes in my sleep I can sense him laying a cloth on my forehead, or clutching my hand when the dreams are too terrible.

Yet in a way I think the dreams are his fault. I dream of the things he has told me, of what it was like to be a slave. I knew those things, of course. But I never thought they made a difference. After all, they were only blacks. They weren't the same as white men.

Now I don't know. I have rarely met a man as fine as Samson Carter.

I am confused.

JUNE 14, 1863

I do not think I will live very long. I have asked the innkeeper to bring me paper.

I have to make a map and a will.

That was the last entry in the diary.

CHAPTER SEVENTEEN

Ruby Fire

I looked up. Through the window I could see the first rays of dawn. My father was going to wonder why we were so tired, when we had gone to bed so early!

I closed the diary and looked at Chris. I was still trying to figure out exactly what it meant. One thing did seem clear: we had an important tool for understanding what was going on at the Quackadoodle. If nothing else, we finally knew why a Rebel ghost was haunting a Yankee inn.

"The way I figure it," said Chris, "old Captain Gray must have died before he could make the map and the will—"

"Wait a minute," I interrupted. "He's not old. He's young!"

"What do you mean?" said Chris. She closed her eyes and did a quick calculation. "The man has to be pushing a hundred and fifty!"

"Sure," I replied. "But I'll bet he wasn't even thirty when he died. So he's young."

That got us going on a discussion about how you should figure a ghost's age. But since neither of us really knew, we finally decided to look it up when we got home.

"Anyway," I said, "I don't see any reason why he couldn't have made the map and the will. The only thing is, they wouldn't have done him any good, unless he could have found some way to pass them on to his Canadian contact. He could hardly ask Samson Carter to help him do that! My guess is that the reason Captain Gray is haunting the inn is because the treasure is still here. It was his responsibility, so he feels he has to guard it."

Chris stopped to think about that. "Makes sense," she said after a minute. Suddenly her eyes opened wide. "Did you hear what you just said?" she asked.

"What?"

"The treasure. It's still here! What if we can find it?"

"But it doesn't belong to us. It belongs to Captain Gray."

"Well, he can't use it," snorted Chris. "He's dead!"

"Shhhh!" I hissed. I looked around nervously. I didn't know if the ghost would like this line of conversation.

"Look, if he doesn't want us to have the treasure, why did he lead us to the diary?" Chris asked defensively.

"I don't know. Maybe he wants us to finish his mission."

"That's silly," said Chris. "The war ended nearly a hundred and twenty-five years ago!"

"Well, maybe he doesn't know that!"

That got us sidetracked again, and we spent the next few minutes trying to figure out how time passes for ghosts, and whether or not they pay attention to current events. It's weird. I've dealt with two ghosts now, which in a way makes me kind of an expert, and I don't have the slightest idea about that kind of thing. I mean, do they read the headlines in the morning paper? If the house they're haunting has a television, do they watch the evening news? Or do they just focus on whatever is keeping them in this world—like this mysterious treasure?

"I wonder if anyone else knows about the treasure?" asked Chris suddenly.

"How could they?"

She shrugged. "I don't know. Some people are real Civil War freaks. I've got an uncle like that. He knows all kinds of weird stories about the war. Maybe it's even in a book somewhere. I bet years later those Charleston women told their kids about how they donated their jewels to the cause only to have them disappear on the way to Canada. Maybe it's a family legend—you know, one of those things that gets passed on from generation to generation."

"Then you think someone here might be looking for it?" I asked.

"Well, that would explain why the plans were stolen from your father's room," said Chris. "If someone came here hoping to find the treasure, and they knew this place had been a stop on the Underground Railroad, they might figure the plans would show some special hiding places—the kind of place where someone might tuck away a treasure."

"But the ghost didn't do that," I said. "He buried it!"

Chris just looked at me.

"Right," I said, feeling silly. "You know that. And I know that. But anyone who hasn't read the diary wouldn't know that."

"I'm glad your brain is working again," said Chris. She went to the dresser and got the ruby. "Come here." She motioned for me to follow her as she crossed to the window.

She held the ruby in her palm. The light of the rising sun caught in the stone. It looked like rose petals, like blood, like fire. Suddenly I wanted it to be all mine.

It was a frightening feeling. That was when I finally understood why so many terrible things happen around treasures like this. I knew there was a part of me that would do any-thing to possess this jewel.

Chris closed her hand, separating the stone from the sunshine. It was like breaking a spell.

She looked at me. I got the feeling she had experienced the same hungry greed that had frightened me.

"We'd better find a safe place to keep this thing," said Chris.

I nodded. Whoever the thief was, he or she might decide that if my father had any more useful information, he would put it in our room for safekeeping. The basic theory would be wrong. But if they searched our room they'd still get results.

"Baltimore probably has a safe," I said. "We can put it in there."

"Good idea. But first let's put it in an envelope or something. Right now the fewer people who know about this, the better." She paused. "I wonder if the treasure belongs to Baltimore," she said. "After all, he owns the inn now."

I shrugged. "Could be. It might depend on where it's buried. Or whether or not we can find the will."

I knew that if the law got involved with this thing, the treasure could be tied up for years while people tried to figure out who had a legal right to it. The thing was, as far as I was concerned it really belonged to Captain Gray. So I figured he was the one who ought to say where it should go. Somehow, I didn't think that would happen if we ended up in court. I could just see us trying to explain to a judge that the ghost of the original owner had told us what to do with the treasure. It would probably get us sent to a room with padded walls.

We were still trying to figure all that out when my father knocked on the door and asked if we were coming to breakfast with him.

We said he'd have to give us time to get ready.

He said that the invitation was for breakfast, not lunch.

We called him a male chauvinist pig, and told him we'd meet him in the dining room in ten minutes. We did, too, although it wasn't easy. I was still trying to get the last knots out of my hair as we walked through the dining room door. I quickly slipped the comb into my pocket when I saw that Mona was sitting at the table with Dad.

I went to get some milk and one of Dieter's pastries. "Maybe the ghost isn't really guarding the treasure after all," I said to Chris. She was standing beside me, dumping sugar in her coffee as if it was the last time she was ever going to see the stuff.

"What do you mean?" she asked.

"Maybe he had one of Dieter's pastries and decided he had already made it to heaven."

"You could be right," she said, putting two of them on her plate. "I'd be perfectly willing to come back here for breakfast every day after I'm dead."

"Well, did you two sleep all right?" my father asked when we sat down.

"Fine," I said—which was quite true for the time we had actually spent sleeping.

Mona looked terrific. That worried me, since I didn't think most women would bother to look that good that early in the morning when they were on vacation, unless they were after some guy. Like my father.

"If I leave you two alone today do you think you can stay out of trouble?" asked Dad.

"Mr. Tanleven!" Chris cried. "How can you even ask such a question?"

My father rolled his eyes. "You're right," he said. "I should know better. Of course you can't stay out of trouble. But I have to go into town to talk to some contractors about the work on the inn, so I'd appreciate it if you could keep things below crisis level here."

"We'll certainly try," I said primly.

"They can always check in with me, Henry," Mona said. "I'll just be loafing around the inn most of the day."

Ah-ha! At least she wasn't going to town with him.

"Excuse me a minute," said Chris, pushing herself away from the table. I wondered where she was going, until I spotted Baltimore on the other side of the room. Then I knew she must be planning to ask him about the safe.

The inn had one, just as we expected. But as it turned out, using it was not one of the smartest things we had ever done.

CHAPTER EIGHTEEN

Over the Hill

After breakfast we borrowed a large brown envelope from my father. I put the diary in it. I was about to add the ruby when Chris said, "Let's take it with us. I like to look at it."

I handed her the stone, and she slipped it into the pocket of her jeans.

Baltimore chuckled when we handed him the envelope. "It'll be safe with me, girls," he said, giving us a wink. He seemed to think we were playing a game, pretending to be international spies or something. That was fine with us. We figured out a long time ago that kids can get away with all kinds of things by being serious. For some reason, it almost always makes a grown-up think you're fooling around.

Once we had the diary locked away, we headed out to the bridge for a little strategy session. We ran into the Deadly Wildflower Bandits on the way.

"Good morning, girls," Meg said. "I hope you slept well."

"Now why do you suppose she said that?" asked Chris, once the Colemans were out of hearing distance.

"She was being polite?"

"Maybe. And maybe she was telling us she knew we had been wandering around in the middle of the night—giving us a warning to keep our noses out of things."

"Don't be ridiculous. Those two are as innocent as we are."

"Maybe," said Chris. "But think for a minute. Where are they from?"

"Canada," I answered. "But what does that . . ."

My voice trailed off as I realized what Chris was saying. If the Colemans were from Canada, it was just possible one of them was a descendent of the mysterious Canadian Connection who never showed up to meet Captain Gray. Or at least showed up too late to do him any good. I realized it was the kind of a story that could easily be passed down through a family. "Did I ever tell you about the time your great-great-granddaddy was supposed to go down to New York State to pick up a fortune in jewels? When he got there, the man he was supposed to meet was dead, and the treasure had disappeared. No one ever found out what happened, but rumor has it he buried the things somewhere on the grounds of the Quackadoodle Inn."

Looking for a treasure like that might make a nice hobby for a retired couple—a hobby they could disguise by pretending they were dig-

ging up wildflowers! Suddenly Meg and Arnie
didn't seem so sweet and innocent after all.

I was still chewing on that when Chris
hissed, "Look, there he is again."

"The ghost?" I asked, surprised that he
would be out in the daylight.

"No, dummy. *Peter.*"

I looked where she was pointing. Peter
Gorham was painting furniture again.

Before I could answer her, Peter spotted us.
He waved his paintbrush in the air, sending an
arc of green paint out in front of him. "Morning,
girls!" he called.

"Think you can keep from embarrassing
yourself?" asked Chris as she started in Peter's
direction.

"I'm willing to try," I answered. I figured
this was a no-lose situation. Even if we couldn't
get any new information from Peter, we'd at
least be able to stand there and look at him for a
while. I wondered how long it would take for
Gloria to spot him talking to us and screech him
back to work.

"I hear your father made a big discovery
yesterday," said Peter when we strolled up to
him.

I nodded. "Seems this place was a stop on
the Underground Railroad," I said.

Peter dipped his brush into the bucket of
paint. "That's hardly news," he said. "This
whole area was a hotbed of antislave activity.
They cram it down your throat over and over
again if you go to school here. That guy Samson

Carter used to live just over the hill there." He
gestured to his right with the paintbrush, spat-
tering more green across the grass. "The county
made his house into a museum. I must have
been dragged there five or six times when I was
in elementary school. I guess our teachers didn't
think we had the brains to go on our own."

"Is it worth the trip?" I asked, feeling
vaguely guilty about all the museums in Syracuse that I had never bothered to visit.

He shrugged. "If you like that kind of stuff.
It's mostly old furniture, plus some pictures and
newspaper clippings. I can take it or leave it."

"Is it open today?" asked Chris.

"Probably. It's Friday, so they can count on
some tourist business."

I was about to ask Peter if he knew anything about a treasure that was supposed to be
buried near the inn when an upstairs window
slid open and a familiar voice shrieked, "Peter
Gorham! You get back to work!"

Peter smiled, which almost made my heart
stop. "You girls better scram, or Gloria will have
my head."

We smiled and scrammed. We didn't even
have to discuss what he had told us. Our next
move was obvious.

Baltimore was glad to give us specific directions to the museum. He even asked Dieter to
pack us a box lunch. At about ten o'clock we
started walking down a country lane carrying
food that would have been a hit in any fancy res-
taurant.

As it turned out Peter's "just over the hill" was more like two miles down the road. But it was a beautiful walk. We even saw a deer along the way.

The Samson Carter house turned out to be a little wooden building surrounded by a picket fence. To the side was a slightly overgrown garden, crowded with flowers and vegetables. A white sign announced the hours the building was open.

We stepped through the gate and walked up to the house, wondering what we might find.

CHAPTER NINETEEN

Samson Carter

A white-haired woman sat on a wooden chair just inside the door. She was fanning herself with a folded-up newspaper. It didn't seem to be doing much good, though; her pale, wrinkled skin still glistened with sweat.

"Morning, girls," she said as we stepped in. "You visiting around here?"

"We're staying at the Quackadoodle," I said.

The woman snorted. "What, over with that crazy Baltimore Cleveland?"

I didn't like her attitude. My first reaction was to defend Baltimore. But I caught myself, realizing we'd probably get more information out of the woman if we just acted casual. So I said, "What's wrong with Baltimore?" as if I didn't really care.

"The man's got no common sense," the woman said, tapping herself on the forehead with her newspaper. "He doesn't know third base from page nine. And he's in debt to just about everyone in the county." She leaned forward. "It wouldn't surprise me if he lost that place before the summer's over."

I swallowed hard at that bit of news. If Baltimore was out of money, how was he going to pay my father?

"Anyway, what brings you girls here?"

"We just heard about the museum," said Chris with a shrug. "We thought it would be fun to take a look at it."

"Well, go ahead and look," the woman said, gesturing with her newspaper. "My name is Effie Calkins. You can call me Effie. If you have any questions, I'll be right here."

She closed her eyes and started fanning herself again.

Trying to keep from giggling, Chris and I began to look around. The room we were in was small and clean. A plaque on the wall said that it had been restored to look the same as it had when Samson Carter lived there a hundred and twenty-five years ago. I assumed that did not include the rack of crummy postcards or the glass counter they sat on.

It was a fascinating little place. We started by going out back, where another little garden was planted with the same flowers and vegetables Samson Carter had once grown on that very spot.

Back inside, we climbed a narrow stairway to a pair of small bedrooms. White curtains, lifted by a passing breeze, floated away from the windows. The bare wooden floor was made of wide boards. The bed in one room was made of tree branches tied together with thin rope. When I put my hand on the mattress it rustled.

"Corn husks," said Effie, when I asked her about it back downstairs. "Folks used to stuff mattresses with them all the time. 'Course, they had to dry them first. But it must have worked all right. At least, I never heard of anyone dying from it. Not that I'd want to try it myself. I'm perfectly happy with my waterbed, thank you very much."

"You have a waterbed?" Chris laughed.

"Anything wrong with that?" Effie sounded offended.

"Are there any secret rooms here?" I asked, partly to change the subject and partly because I had been trying to see if I could spot one since we had first entered the place.

It was Effie's turn to laugh. "This wouldn't have been the best place for Samson to hide folks," she said. "He was too well known."

I felt a little silly. I also felt a little angry with Effie for making me feel so silly. I didn't think it was such a bad question to ask. I wish people wouldn't do that when you ask a question. It makes it hard to ask the next one. Sometimes you'd rather stay stupid than have someone laugh at you.

I think Effie realized what she had done because she went behind the counter and got out a book. "Here," she said, "you girls might like to look at this. It's a biography of Samson Carter. Tells all kinds of interesting things about him; that man did more good works on an off day than two parsons and a politician generally manage in a lifetime."

"Can we sit on the porch and look at this?" asked Chris.

"I suppose so," Effie said. "As long as you promise not to run off with it."

When we opened the book, it looked weird. I couldn't figure out why, until I realized that the words on the right edge of each page formed a zigzag pattern, instead of a straight line, like most books. The pages looked more like a type-written letter than a regular book.

We flipped to the front. According to the copyright page, the book had been written by someone who lived near Samson Carter, and pub-lished by a local company. I was used to regular books; it was strange to see something like this.

We began to read. It was fascinating—all about the terrible things that had happened to Samson Carter when he was a young slave, and the enormous risks he had taken to escape from slavery. I found myself wondering if I would have had the courage to endure all that to seek my own freedom.

Then it talked about his work with the Un-derground Railroad. I wish I had room to write about some of his adventures. There were so many disguises, chases, daring escapes, close calls—But he never lost one of his people, even though getting them out almost cost him his own life more than once—like the time he ran into a swamp to lead a pack of hunting hounds away from the rest of his group and almost got caught in quicksand.

And then we found the map. It was in the center of the book, tucked in with about twenty pages of photographs and drawings of Samson Carter and the other people and places mentioned in the book. We might have flipped right by it, if I hadn't noticed the words "Cap'n Gray" written at the top.

"Whoa!" I yelled as Chris started to turn the page. She stopped, and we stared at it for a minute, trying to make sense of it. It looked vaguely familiar.

"Is there a caption?" I asked finally. Chris turned the page. The next page had two photographs of people Samson Carter had rescued. There were three captions, one for each of the photos, and one that said, "Overleaf: map found among Samson Carter's papers after his death, indicating the burial place of Captain Jonathan Gray. See story, on page 155."

We flipped back to the map. Sure enough, it showed the location of the little cemetery we had found near the waterfall.

We turned to page 155. The first part of the story was the author's version of stuff we already knew from Captain Gray's diary. Then it got more interesting. According to the story Samson Carter told the author, Captain Gray had just started to make his will when the searchers came looking for him again. So Carter and the innkeeper had taken the captain back to the hidden room.

It was an hour before the men left. Captain Gray's last hour on earth, as it turned out; he was dead when the innkeeper went back to get him.

That was sad enough. But the rest of the book was even sadder, because it told the story of Samson Carter's death. I had just assumed that since he had survived running the Underground Railroad, he must have lived on to die a peaceful death.

The world doesn't work that way, I guess. It turns out that he had made many trips to the South during the war, serving the Union sometimes as a spy, sometimes as a scout. That was incredibly dangerous, of course, but he used all his contacts and tricks from the days on the Underground and managed to survive it all.

He was an old man by that time. The drawings and photos of him were wonderful—you could see both his sweetness and his strength. I guess you would have needed both those qualities to do everything that Samson Carter did.

Anyway, six months after the war ended, Samson Carter went to the South as a free man, traveling there legally for the first time in over thirty years. He went to visit some friends, and to begin planning his great dream: the Samson Carter Institute, a college for the children of former slaves. The trip was a success. But while he was on his way home he passed through a town where a mob of angry men beat him to death.

They didn't kill him because he was Samsom Carter and had worked so hard to free so many slaves.

They didn't even know who he was.

They just killed him because he was black.

CHAPTER TWENTY

Crisis Level

We walked back to the Quackadoodle in silence, each of us wrapped in our own thoughts. So much had happened, and so long ago. How did it all fit together?

We did have one more piece of good luck at the museum. When we took the book back to Effie, we were so enthusiastic about it that she showed us a thin little paperback the museum sold as a souvenir. "Don't sell many of these," she said. "They're about as popular as termites in a lumberyard. So I don't bother to show it to folks. But since you seem so interested—"

So for two dollars we had a small version of the Samson Carter story, complete with illustrations.

It was late afternoon when we finally made it back to the inn. I wanted to check on some things in Captain Gray's diary so Chris and I went into the lobby. It was empty. We rang the bell, but no one came. We stood there for a moment, feeling hot and impatient.

"Come on," said Chris. "Let's check the office. For all we know Baltimore's in there listening to Bruce Springsteen on a Walkman. Probably he just couldn't hear us ring."

The idea seemed unlikely to me, but I followed her, anyway. As it turned out, Chris was about half-right. Baltimore was in the office. But he wasn't listening to Springsteen. He was lying face down on the floor with his eyes closed. We could see a purple swelling the size of a baby's fist on the back of his head.

The safe, which was normally hidden behind a painting, was wide open. It was also completely empty.

Chris, who is not as squeamish about these things as I am, bent down and put her ear against Baltimore's back.

"He's alive," she said. "Just unconscious. I'll stay with him. You go get help."

I could feel my hands begin to shake as I left the office. Ghosts were one thing. Whoever had bopped Baltimore was flesh and blood, and playing for real. Suddenly this mystery didn't seem like such a game anymore.

The first person I found was Gloria. She was kneeling in front of a wooden table, polishing it with an oily cloth. I wasn't sure what I should say. After all, it was *her* husband lying on the floor in there. I tried to stay calm. "Gloria, I need some help."

"I'm sure it can wait," she said. "You can see I'm busy now."

That made me angry. "It's Baltimore," I said sharply. "He's been hurt!"

What a transformation! The only other time I've seen anyone get to his feet so fast was one evening when I was watching TV with Chris and her brothers and Mrs. Gurley yelled "Dinner!" All six of those boys were on their feet and into the dining room before I had managed to un- cross my legs.

Gloria moved the same way now. "Where is he?" she asked.

I told her, then hurried to keep up as she charged down the hallway.

Baltimore was starting to regain con- sciousness when we entered the office. He had rolled over onto his back. Chris was sitting be- side him, holding his shoulders. He opened and closed his eyes a few times, moaning gently as he did so.

Gloria knelt beside him. "What happened, sweetie?" she asked, kissing him on his bald spot.

He groaned, but didn't answer her.

Gloria sent me to call a doctor—and the po- lice. Before we knew it there were six deputies swarming all over the place and getting in one another's way.

"Too much time, too little crime," said Mona, who had come to see what the commotion was all about. "The only thing worse than hav- ing the police department bored is having them overworked."

The police wanted to talk to us, of course. They asked about how we had found Baltimore. We told them. They asked what we did next. We told them. But they didn't ask if we had anything in the safe ourselves. So we didn't tell them—mostly because we had talked it over before the police got to us, and neither one of us believed that Captain Gray wanted the police involved in this thing.

My father came in while we were giving our statements. He took one look at the scene—Chris and I sitting and talking to a cop with a notebook—rolled his eyes, and walked over to Mona. I could imagine what he was saying: "All I asked them to do was keep things below crisis level. Was that so much to ask? Was it?"

But I didn't feel too guilty. I figured we didn't have anything to do with this.

I was almost right, too.

Dinner that night was a quiet affair. Everyone in the inn wanted to believe that whoever attacked Baltimore had been an outsider. But everyone also knew that it might have been one of the guests. My father gave us several warnings about not getting too nosy and so on. He wanted to know how much we knew about what was going on. But since I didn't figure things out until later in the evening, I could honestly tell him, "not much."

By nine o'clock more than half the couples that had come for the weekend had checked out. Things looked pretty bad for the big dance the next night.

In fact, they looked pretty bad for the Quackadoodle in general. Between what Porter had told us earlier and what Effie had said that afternoon, I was pretty worried about the fact that my father had quit his job on the basis of what he expected to make from Baltimore. I was trying to figure out what I should say to him about it as Chris and I climbed the stairs to go to our room.

I stopped across from the picture of Captain Gray. "What do *you* think I should do about all this?"

The picture didn't answer me, of course. But as I stood there looking at it something else occurred to me.

"You know, there's something odd about this picture," I said.

"I don't think so," said Chris. "He looks just as good in real life, or real death, or whatever."

"Yeah, but what's it doing here? I mean, when we first saw it, I thought it was just an old picture they had hung here because it sort of went with the inn. But it really has a connection to the place."

"I see what you mean," said Chris. "Captain Gray wouldn't have had his photo taken while he was here, at least not in uniform. So where did it come from?"

I reached up to take the photo off the wall.

"What are you doing?" asked Chris. She sounded nervous.

"Calm down," I said, setting the frame on the floor. "I just want to see if there's any writing on the back."

Chris knelt beside me. I turned the frame around and sighed. The back of the picture was covered with plain brown paper; it was discolored in some spots, and tearing away from the edge of the frame in others. But there was no writing on it at all.

"Oh, well," said Chris. "It was a good idea."

I was picking the picture up to put it back when I noticed a bit of white paper under one of the torn spots. I set the frame back down and ran my fingers over the brown paper. Then I started picking at it, tearing it off in tiny bits.

"What are you doing?" asked Chris.

"I think there's something under here," I said.

"Nine, you can't do that. We'll get in trouble."

We all have our weak spots. Chris is brave; without blinking an eye she'll walk into places that I would rather run from. But she doesn't like getting in trouble with grown-ups.

"Who's going to know?" I said. Then I peeled away a larger strip of the paper.

"Jackpot!" whispered Chris.

Underneath the paper, taped to the back of the picture, was a yellowed envelope.

I pulled away the rest of the paper that covered the envelope. Working carefully, because the envelope itself was brittle, I removed it from the picture.

I turned it over. It was addressed to "Richard Farnsworth, Innkeeper, The Quackadoodle Inn."

"Hurry up and open it!" Chris whispered.

I shook my head. "Take it," I said, thrusting the envelope into her hands. I stood up to replace the picture.

Just in time! We heard someone whistling, and Porter Markson appeared at the top of the stairs just as I was straightening the frame.

He gave me a funny look. "Admiring the ghost?" he asked.

I smiled, trying to look innocent. "He's just so good-looking," I said.

"She's got a crush," said Chris, who was leaning against the wall with her hands behind her back to hide the envelope.

I shot Chris a nasty glare. Porter chuckled. "Ah, to be young again," he said and wandered down the hall.

"You didn't have to say that," I hissed when he was out of earshot.

Chris grinned. "It threw him off the track," she said. "Come on. Let's get to our room and look at that letter."

We scooted down the hall. But when we got to our room we met Isabella coming out of the door.

"What timing," she said, smiling brightly. "Your room is all set."

She walked away, whistling cheerfully. Chris and I stepped inside, closed the door behind us, and looked at each other.

"Was she really cleaning up in here?" I asked. "Or was she snooping around?"

"I don't know," said Chris. "Remember that speech in the kitchen yesterday? She seemed to know an awful lot about some of the stuff that's gone on here in the past."

"And she's got keys for all the rooms," I said, following that line of thought. "Do you think she could be the one who stole the plans?"

"It's possible. She and Martha had a lot of time when no one was watching them that evening. I wonder if the two of them are in this together?"

My head was starting to spin. "Let's think about that later," I said. "Right now I want to take a look at this!"

Trying not to tear the brittle old paper, I opened the envelope we had found behind Captain Gray's picture.

Here's the letter we found inside.

SEPTEMBER 12, 1875

Dear Innkeeper Farnsworth:

We would like to thank you for your help in locating the grave of Captain Jonathan Gray. It was a wonderful stroke of luck when you found that map. It meant a great deal to us to be able to provide our friend with the kind of memorial he deserved.

Because of this assistance, and because your predecessor was so kind to Captain Gray while he was alive, caring for him during his illness, and providing him with a decent burial, we would like you to have the enclosed portrait of the captain. Perhaps the sad story that goes with it will prove of interest to your guests.

> Sincerely,
> *The Friends of Captain Jonathan Gray*

"That must be the tombstone we saw in the cemetery," Chris said. "People must have really cared about him, to worry about bringing in a tombstone so long after he had died."

I nodded in agreement.

It wasn't until the middle of the night that I finally figured out what was wrong with the whole situation.

CHAPTER TWENTY-ONE

Grave Undertaking

I sat up in bed. "Chris, wake up."

She sprang to a sitting position. "Is he here?" she asked eagerly. She looked around for Captain Gray.

"No one's here but me," I said, feeling cranky.

"Then why did you wake me up?" She sounded even crankier than I felt.

"Because I know where the treasure is. At least, I think I do."

She turned and looked at me with new interest. "Where?"

I told her.

First she laughed. Then she told me I was crazy.

I explained my reasons.

She still thought I was crazy. But she didn't sound quite so certain.

"Anyway," I said, "we have to go get it. Now."

That pushed her the other way; now she was sure I was crazy. "Permanently around the bend," as she put it.

"But don't you see?" I persisted. "We can't possibly dig it up in the daytime. If anyone ever caught us, we'd get in incredible trouble."

"With good reason. It's sick!"

"No, it's not. Captain Gray wants us to locate the treasure. I'm sure of it."

"Well, why don't we just get someone to dig it up for us? We'll tell them what you figured out, and . . ." Her voice trailed off. Chris knew as well as I did that no grown up was going to go dig up a hundred and twenty-five-year-old grave just because some eleven-year-old kid thought there was a treasure buried in it.

It was us, or no one.

"Well," said Chris, swinging her legs over the edge of the bed, "if we're going to do it, we might as well do it now."

Me and my big mouth! I was so happy about figuring out where the treasure was, I hadn't really thought about what it would mean if we decided to go get it. Now that I had Chris all excited, I started to realize just what I had gotten myself into.

I made a resolution: I will, I will, I *will* learn to keep my mouth shut.

I kept repeating it to myself as we pulled on our jeans, sweatshirts, and sneakers. I continued repeating it as we sneaked down the stairs. I began to think about having it tattooed on my forehead as we made our way across the lawn to the toolshed where we had seen Peter store the mower and paint cans.

"Well," said Chris when she opened the doors, "looks like we can find just about anything we need in here."

"The trick will be getting it out once we find it," I said, staring inside.

Did you ever play Pick Up Sticks? Imagine that game played with two-by-fours, old rakes, broken shovels, and eight-foot crowbars, and you'll have some idea of what the inside of the shed looked like. Now imagine trying to pick your way through a mess like that without making any noise.

I should have stayed in bed.

We stepped in. I pointed the flashlight here and there, looking for what we needed. At one point my foot got stuck in a hole in the floor. I was still trying to figure out how I was going to explain to my father why I was trapped in the toolshed when Chris pried me loose.

"Come on," she said. "I think we've got what we need."

She was wrong, of course. What we needed was someone to talk some sense into us! But since I was the one who started this whole expedition, I had no one to blame but myself.

Carrying two shovels, a pick, and a long metal rod, we headed for the graveyard.

The full moon was brighter, more clear, than I had ever seen it in the city. It flooded the lawn with silver light. The effect was strange. It was dark, but not dark; I could see Chris's face very clearly. But in the strange midnight light she looked almost like a ghost herself.

We crossed the bridge. The water seemed quieter, as if it knew not to make too much noise that late at night.

Once we entered the woods we needed our flashlights. The moonlight only filtered down in patches and puddles, scattered among the shadows. It was almost soundless. Everything smelled moist.

The silence ended when we had gone far enough to hear the waterfall. The sound was comforting.

We stopped at the head of the falls, because they were too beautiful to pass. The water splashing and tumbling over the cliff almost seemed to be made of light. I could feel the cool spray on my face. I looked down to where the stream splashed against the dark rocks, some forty feet below. The moonlight made the spray look like a net of tiny pearls.

"Don't stand so close to the edge," said Chris in one of her rare sensible moments. "It's a long way down."

I had a momentary vision of slipping over the edge of the cliff and bouncing off the rocks far below. I swallowed and stepped back from the edge. "We'd better get moving," I said. "We don't know how long this is going to take."

"Right," said Chris.

Less than two minutes later we were standing in the little cemetery. Now I was really nervous. What kind of things lurked in a cemetery at night? Every tombstone had a dark shadow. Every shadow might be hiding something awful. I pointed my flashlight this way and that, smashing the shadows. I don't know what I expected to find. Certainly it was better to find nothing. Yet I had a uneasy sensation that we were being watched.

"Maybe it's Captain Gray," said Chris when I mentioned the feeling.

I didn't know if that made me feel better or not.

I decided we should start digging.

"Just where did you have in mind, Sherlock?" Chris asked. I could tell by the tone in her voice that for all her acting brave, she didn't think this was the most wonderful thing that had ever happened to her.

I bit my lip. "If the family followed the map carefully, the treasure should be right under the stone."

I went to Captain Gray's headstone and looked around. I figured the dead tree at the edge of the clearing was the one shown on the map.

"Give me that tape measure," I said to Chris.

She fished the tape we had found in the toolshed out of her pocket. I took one end of it, and told her to walk to the tree.

She did as I asked, muttering to herself as she picked her way through the bushes.

When she reached the tree, she stretched the tape tight. "Twenty-five feet," she said, squinting to make out the numbers.

I frowned. "It should be twenty-three."

Chris began walking back toward me, rolling up the tape as she came. "What did you expect—that we would hit it right on the nose? I doubt Captain Gray was using a ruler when he measured this. Probably he just paced it off. Besides that old tree must have grown a foot or two since he used it as a marker."

"This could end up being one big hole," I said nervously.

Then another thought occurred to me. "Do you think his friends would have put the gravestone exactly on the spot marked on the map? Or would they have moved it to one side, figuring it should go at the head of the grave?"

Chris tilted her head to one side and thought. "If it was me, I would have put it right on the spot," she said finally. "If you were trying for the head of the grave, or something fancy like that, you might miss it altogether."

"Well, shall we start?" I said.

She looked at me. She looked at the tombstone. She swallowed, hard.

"Let's do it," she whispered.

I learned a whole new respect for grave diggers that night. It's hard work! First we had to cut through the undergrowth. We took turns, one of us whacking away at the plants while the other held the flashlight.

"We should have brought an ax," I said after a few minutes of trying to hack my way through a burdock root with the tip of the spade.

"Live and learn," said Chris. It seemed like a weird thing to say, considering where we were

and what we were doing. I gave her the spade
and took the flashlight.

"I'm glad this place doesn't have many vis-
itors," she panted after about half an hour. "I
don't care how carefully we clean up, this is *not*
going to look like it did when we started."

I looked around at the mess we had made
and nodded. If I was right, it wouldn't make any
difference. If I was wrong—well, I didn't want to
think about what would happen if I was wrong.

She came and stood beside me. I played the
flashlight over the hole.

"What next, Fearless Leader—do we make
it wider, or deeper?"

How was I supposed to know? "Deeper," I
said at last.

Chris made a face. "I was afraid of that. I
don't want to think about what we might find if
you're wrong."

An ugly image flashed into my mind. I
pushed it away. It was too awful to think about.
Besides, I was feeling more and more confident
that I was on the right track. I figured if it was
really Captain Gray's body buried here, instead
of the treasure, his ghost would have showed up
to warn us off.

We dug deeper. We dug wider.

A cool breeze came and went, playing
through the ends of our hair like ghostly fingers. Were other spirits lurking here in this old
cemetery? An owl began hooting somewhere off
to our right.

We decided to do some probing. Using the metal rod we had brought from the toolshed, we began poking at the soil.

A pattern began to develop: poke, poke, poke; nothing, nothing; *clunk*. We'd dig for the clunk and find a rock. After a while we realized that if we poked the rod on either side of the clunk, we could sometimes figure out if it was too small to be the treasure box, and save ourselves a little digging.

We were both standing in the hole now. It was almost three feet deep and went straight down from the front edge of the gravestone.

I was noticing that I had enough dirt under my fingernails to start a small garden when it occurred to me that the treasure might be right under the stone.

That would make things difficult.

"Step out for a minute," I said to Chris.

She climbed out of the hole. That gave me enough room to squat down and poke the rod into the soil under the stone.

Six inches in on the first try I heard a *clunk*!

I moved the rod to the right. *Clunk*.

I moved it to the left. *Clunk*.

I tried it three inches higher. Nothing. Three inches down. Nothing. I could feel my heart begin to pound. This looked like it might be it!

Using the tip of the rod I began to pull away the soil. When that was too slow, I switched to using my hands. I could always clean my nails later. Finally I felt something smooth and cool, too smooth to be a rock.

"I think I've got it!" I cried.

I pulled away more soil. There it was—the metal box!

I let out a shout of joy as I dug the box out of the damp soil. "Chris, we did it!"

But Chris didn't answer. Instead I heard a familiar voice say, "Good work, Nine. Why don't you hand me the box. Then you can get out of the hole."

I looked up. Porter Markson was standing at the edge of the hole, looking down at me. Chris was standing next to him. Porter had one hand on her arm. His other hand was holding a gun. It was pointing at her head.

CHAPTER TWENTY-TWO

Revenant

"Well, fancy meeting you here," I said, trying to sound casual.

"Shut up," said Porter, "or your friend gets an air-conditioned brain."

I shut up. I put the box at Porter's feet as he directed. Then I climbed slowly out of the hole.

I was trying to think, but I was too frightened. I was even too scared to get mad. But I wanted to. Who did this guy think he was, to come and take the treasure after we had done all the work?

Besides, how did he think he was going to get away with it? He wasn't even wearing a mask. We would just tell the police who had done it, and . . .

I may be a little slow, but I'm not entirely stupid. It was about then that I realized Porter probably had no intention of letting us tell anything to anyone. Odds were, he did not intend to let either one of us live to see the morning.

"The thing is, how to do it," he said as if he were reading my mind. "It's a little like one of those problems where you have to get a fox, a goose, and a sack of grain across the river without anything getting eaten, even though you can only take one thing across at a time. Now in this case, there are two of you, and only one of me. Fortunately, I have a gun. Unfortunately, I can't simply shoot you and get it over with. No, that would raise too many questions."

"That's a real problem," I said. "Maybe we should all just go home."

Porter smiled. "You're a cute kid, Nine. It's a shame your father didn't discipline you better. He'll feel terrible when he finds out you fell over the waterfall. But what can a man expect, when he lets his kids wander around in the middle of the night like this?"

This guy was good. I could see the whole plan at once: Chris and I don't show up for breakfast—my father panics—a search party gets formed—and several hours later they find the two of us lying at the bottom of the falls. Everyone shakes his head and *tsk-tsks* about what reckless kids we were, and how that kind of craziness always leads to tragedy. Or even worse, they decide it was a mutual suicide pact. That really made me mad. If I had to die, I didn't want people thinking it was because I was dumb enough to kill myself!

"There's some rope beside that tree," said Porter, motioning with his head. "Go get it."

I did as he told me. Then he directed Chris to stand against the tree, while I tied her up.

"Not taking any chances, are you?" I said.

Porter shook his head. "I've waited too long for this moment."

"Is that why you've been coming here all these years?" I asked.

"It's a family tradition," said Porter.

"Hanging around graveyards?" I asked. It was a smart-mouth thing to say. But I figured I couldn't get in any more trouble than I was already.

Porter smiled. I suppose it's easy to be tolerant when you're the one holding the gun. "Not hanging around cemeteries," he said. "Looking for Captain Gray's treasure."

Ah-ha! I thought. *Here's where things start to fall into place.*

"How long has this been going on?" asked Chris.

Porter shrugged. "Personally, about thirty years. But my family's been at it, off and on, for nearly a hundred and twenty-five."

When I heard that, things didn't just fall into place; they came together with a crash like two speeding cars having a head-on collision.

I looked at Porter. He stood in the center of the clearing, bathed in moonlight, his face smiling happily. If it hadn't been for the gun in his hand he would have looked almost angelic.

"The man who killed Captain Gray was an ancestor of yours, wasn't he?" I asked.

Porter nodded.

"Doesn't that embarrass you?" asked Chris.

"Don't be ridiculous," said Porter. "We were at war. Johnny Gray was an enemy agent."

"Was your ancestor a soldier?" I asked.

"What difference does that make?" he snapped.

It seemed to me that it made a big difference; from the way Captain Gray's diary read, whoever had killed him was more interested in the treasure than in doing his patriotic duty. But I decided it wasn't necessarily a good idea to mention that right then.

"All right. Now you go over there and sit down," said Porter as I finished tying Chris to the tree. He waved his gun to the right. I did as he told me.

"The thing is," he said as he went to the tree to check my knots, "even though my ancestor couldn't find the treasure, he knew it was here. So every year he brought his family for a vacation, and while they played, he tried to figure out where the treasure was. Poor old codger. He never thought to look in the captain's grave. After he died it was just a game with most of the family. They came here every year for their vacation, and talked about the treasure. But no one did much of anything about it. Until me. I was the first one in a long time to take it seriously. But even after I stole the diary today, I couldn't figure out where it was. So tell me— how did *you* figure it out?"

I wasn't particularly eager to tell him. On the other hand, he did have a gun.

"It was something we saw at the Samson Carter museum that started putting it together for me," I said. "They had a map with Captain

Gray's name written on the top. Then we found a letter on the back of Captain Gray's picture that indicated his friends had used the map to locate the captain's grave when they decided to put on the headstone."

"So what?"

"Well, that made some sense, until I started putting together the dates on the letter and the diary. Then I realized that the map must have been the one that Captain Gray had made to show Samson where the treasure was. Samson left the map with his family, figuring he would come back and get the treasure later. But then he was killed in Virginia. His family didn't know about the treasure. When Captain Gray's friends contacted them, they remembered a map with Captain Gray's name on it, and assumed it showed where he was buried. When I realized their mistake, I figured all we had to do was dig around the headstone, and we would find the treasure."

"Very clever," said Porter, stepping up to the tree. He looked down at the rope and made a clucking sound. "Nice try, Nine," he said. "Now come back here and tie this right. And remember—next time I won't be so understanding."

I sighed. Even while I was tying those fake knots I had figured Porter would probably check them. But I also figured it couldn't hurt to try.

"Sorry," I whispered to Chris as I retied the knots. And I was sorry. Having her get loose had been my only hope. Now I was very frightened.

It didn't look as if there was any way out of this mess. A cold chill passed over me as I remembered the view from the edge of the falls.

"OK," said Porter, "back where you were." He motioned with his gun again. Then he bent down to pick up the box.

Suddenly a terrible howling ripped through the clearing. The hair on the back of my neck rose up, and I felt a wave of prickles skitter from my shoulders down to my toes.

Porter stood up so fast it seemed as if someone had grabbed him by the hair and yanked him to his feet. He had the box in one hand, the gun in the other.

Then Captain Gray shimmered into view. But this was not the sweet, sorrowful ghost that Chris and I had come to know. This was a new Captain Gray, an angry, vengeful spirit whose tormented howling seemed to shred the night.

Porter's eyes went wide with terror. "D-d-don't!" he stammered. "Get away! Stay back!"

He fired two shots directly at the ghost. Nothing happened.

The misty form of Captain Gray continued to move forward. His angry howls grew louder. I couldn't see his face. From the look of terror in Porter's eyes, I was just as glad.

Suddenly the ghost raised his hands and reached out for Porter.

"Get back!" screamed the man. "Get back!"

But it was Porter who stepped back. As he did, his foot went over the edge of the hole. He threw his hands upward. But it was too late. His balance was gone. He grabbed at the air, trying to save himself from falling. The gun went flying off to his right. The metal box flipped off to the left. The rusted latch gave way, and a shower of jewels went cascading through the moonlight.

Porter landed on his back in the hole we had dug. He rolled over and crawled forward, trying to scramble out.

Captain Gray's tombstone, already unstable because of the hole I had made underneath it, tottered and tipped forward.

Porter screamed once. Then everything was silent.

The stillness was so intense it was as if the night itself was holding its breath. After a while I realized I had been holding mine. I let it out, and as if on a signal, the breeze began to whisper through the clearing once again.

The owl cried once and then was silent.

Captain Gray turned in our direction. All the anger and ferocity I had sensed before was gone. As he had done that night in our room, he tipped his hat and bowed. He blew us a kiss, then faded into the night.

I untied Chris. Together, holding hands, we walked across the graveyard and peered down into the hole. It was filled from side to side, with the monument erected to Captain Gray.

But the body underneath the stone belonged to Porter Markson.

CHAPTER TWENTY-THREE

The Handwriting on the Wall

The pile of jewels in the middle of the table blazed like a fire. Its flames weren't just red and yellow, either, but green and blue and purple and a lot of other colors as well. I stared at it, thinking it was the kind of thing you might get to see once in a lifetime, and then only if you were lucky.

"Amazing!" said Baltimore. He thrust his stubby hands into the pile of jewels and let them run through his fingers in multicolored streams.

With the exception of Porter, everyone we had met that first day at the Quackadoodle was gathered in the dining room to examine the treasure and hear our story.

Arnie and Meg were sitting side by side. As usual, they were holding hands. They looked so sweet that I felt embarrassed about ever having suspected them. I reminded myself that a good detective has to examine all the alternatives. My father was sitting beside them. Mona stood behind him, resting a hand on his shoulder. Peter and Dieter and Martha and Isabella were standing in a knot to my right. Gloria was beside Baltimore. Her eyes seemed small and hard, and they glittered like jewels themselves, but without any of the warmth of the stones.

"Now tell us all about how you girls figured this out," Meg said. She squeezed Arnie's hand. "Isn't this thrilling, dear?" she whispered.

I glanced at my father. He nodded, so I launched into the story, ghost and all, right up to the point where I put together the information from the diary and the map and the letter on the back of Captain Gray's picture to come up with my idea about where the treasure was hidden.

"It didn't seem that likely that they would have made a map of where they buried Captain Gray," I said. "You put a marker on the grave, but you don't bother to make a map. And it didn't really make sense to me that they would have buried him way up in the woods like that. But I knew from the diary that Captain Gray had been planning to make a map, and it seemed likely that he would have passed it on to Samson Carter. Once I had figured that out, I realized that the map Captain Gray's friends had used to place his headstone didn't show the grave at all, but where the treasure was buried."

"But how did Porter know what you were up to?" asked Meg.

I was silent for a minute, thinking of the

ambulance that had come, and remembering
the men walking out of the woods carrying a
stretcher with the still form of Porter Markson beneath a white sheet. He had been planning on killing us. Yet it was hard to forget the
funny little man who told jokes and played the
piano.

While I was brooding, Chris picked up the
story. "The way we figure it, Porter suspected we
knew something from the beginning—partly
because Mr. Tanleven had the plans to the inn."
She turned to my father. "I don't think he really
believed you were here to do a renovation, Mr. T.
He thought Baltimore had hired you to find the
treasure!"

"So it was Porter who stole the blueprints,"
Mona said.

"Of course," Chris said. "Remember that
first night at dinner, when he told us he usually
stayed in Mr. T's room? Our guess is he had used
the room so often he had his own key. It was easy
for him to get in without any fuss."

"He really thought I was after the treasure?" said my father with a chuckle.

I picked up the story. "He sure did. But you
weren't the only one he was suspicious of. He
was worried about Arnie and Meg, too."

The Coleman's looked astonished. Then Arnie laughed. "I've got it," he said. "It's because
we were always going out into the woods with
our shovels."

Chris nodded. "He was afraid you had found

some clue he didn't know about. Anyway, once he found out about the diary, he was convinced Nine and I knew where the treasure was. He was still awake, studying the diary for the clue, when we went out to get the treasure. He saw us through his window and decided to follow us."

"But how did he know about the diary to begin with?" asked my father. "You two didn't tell anyone you had found it." I could tell from the tone in his voice he was a little hurt about that. I thought about explaining that he was too tied up with Mona to listen to our problems, but decided we should save that discussion for later. Besides, I wasn't sure that was entirely true. I liked doing this kind of stuff on my own. At least, I do as long as Chris is with me. So maybe I wouldn't have told him, anyway.

Baltimore saved me from having to answer by stepping in with a confession of his own. "I told him," he said, blushing fiercely.

Chris and I looked at him. Our faces must have shown how betrayed we felt, because he rushed on to make an explanation.

"I know it was wrong," he said. "But the two of you were so cute with your little games and your mysterious packages, that I couldn't resist opening it to see what was inside."

Cute! Yuck. Now I was really upset with Baltimore.

He shook his head. "Bad, bad Baltimore. I really shouldn't have done that. Then I made things worse by telling Porter about the diary. I only did it because I knew how interested he was in the history of the inn."

He touched the lump on his head ruefully. "I think you'll agree that I paid dearly for my sins. I had no idea Porter's interest in the Quackadoodle was such a greedy one."

"I'm confused about the ghost," said Meg. "I thought ghosts were bound to a specific place—like the inn. How could he pop up at the cemetery like that."

This time Mona stepped in with an answer. "Different things hold different ghosts," she said. "Captain Gray's ghost was tied to the fate of the treasure. Beyond that, he had accepted an obligation to the girls by seeking their help, which he pretty clearly did, even without speaking a word. So when they were in danger, he was able to come to their aid."

"But why us? How come he never asked anyone for help before?" asked Chris.

"How do you know he didn't?" said Mona. "Maybe he tried, but everyone else was too frightened. Maybe he gave up after a while. That would explain why there were a lot of stories about people seeing the ghost a long time ago, but fewer and fewer as the years went on. From what you've said, he didn't expect the two of you to see him. I think that your experience with the Woman in White probably made you more sensitive to seeing ghosts."

My father groaned. "Oh, great. Does that

mean the two of them are going to go on seeing ghosts for the rest of their lives?"

Mona laughed. "I couldn't begin to say, Henry. But I wouldn't worry about it too much. The girls seem to handle themselves rather well."

My father rolled his eyes. "There's a difference between living through something and handling it well."

"The thing that I don't understand," continued Mona, "is who the treasure belongs to. Is it Baltimore's, because it was on his property? Or does it belong to the girls, since they found it?"

"Neither," said Isabella. She shook her head. Little things—a tremor in her hand, the way she forced herself to take a deep breath before she spoke—made me think this was hard for her. She was a quiet person, and she was trying to be very strong now.

"What are you talking about?" asked Gloria. There was ice in her voice.

Isabella took another deep breath. "The treasure belongs to the Samson Carter Institute. It's the college Samson Carter was starting when he was killed."

Chris and I had read about the college. It was one of the reasons that Samson Carter had made his last trip to the South. He was coming back from the first meeting of the board of directors when he was killed.

"Mr. Carter's will left everything he had to

the college," continued Isabella, "including something he called the Quackadoodle Treasure. Only until now, no one knew what the Quackadoodle Treasure was."

She looked around apologetically. "I teach at Samson Carter. I believe in the school. It's an important place. I applied for work here because the college is almost bankrupt, and I hoped I might be able to locate the treasure somehow. It seemed like a long shot. But it also seemed to be our only chance."

"That's very touching," said Gloria. "But just because Samson Carter left your school the treasure in his will doesn't mean that it's yours. I don't see that it was his to give."

"According to Mr. Carter, Captain Gray gave him the treasure in his own will."

"Has anyone ever seen that will?" asked Gloria.

Isabella shook her head. Tears formed in the corners of her eyes. She could see the future of her school in the fiery pile of jewels on the table. In her heart she believed it belonged to the institute. But she had no way to prove it.

Everyone started talking at once.

It was a sticky situation. The school needed the money. Baltimore needed the money. *We* needed the money, for that matter, since we were going to be broke if Baltimore couldn't pay my father.

It would have been nice to just let things

rest; as finders of the treasure Chris and I would certainly get a big share of it. But I figured we had an obligation to Captain Gray to see that the money went where he wanted it to go. Besides, if I was right, it would come out sooner or later anyway.

So I opened my big mouth. "I think I know where Captain Gray's will is," I said.

No one heard me. They were all talking too loud. I tried again, at the top of my lungs. That shut everyone up.

"Where is it?" my father asked.

I told them what we had read in the book about Captain Gray's death. Then I took them into the kitchen. Dieter started squawking as soon as we headed for the door, but Gloria told him to shut up.

I had my father take the patch off the hole he had made in the wall.

Baltimore brought a flashlight. By shining it in at the right angle, he was able to read the words that Captain Gray had scrawled on the wall with a piece of charcoal a hundred and twenty-five years ago. The words he had pointed to the day Chris and I saw him sitting there. The words he had written in the hour of his death.

I, Jonathan Gray, being of sound mind but dying body, and having no living relatives, do hereby bequeath all my worldly goods to the godliest man I have ever had the privilege to meet, Samson Carter. This shall include, as the law allows, the jewels that

I have carried into this state, which were given to wage war, but with the grace of God may be used to teach peace.

> May God rest my soul.
> Captain Jonathan Gray
> June 14, 1863
> In the hour of his death.

Baltimore turned around. "Well," he said softly. "That's that."

Everyone was very quiet.

CHAPTER TWENTY-FOUR

The Glory Road

That night Chris and I put on our best dresses and went down to the dining room for the dance. Baltimore and Peter had rearranged things earlier in the day, to clear the center of the room for dancing. As we entered I saw a row of chairs against the right wall. To our left were several linen-covered tables, piled high with heaping trays of goodies Dieter had whipped up for the event. The table closest to us held an enormous punch bowl filled with clear red liquid. A small band had set up their instruments near the doors that led out onto the porch.

It was all very elegant. I felt kind of grown-up, and a little scared.

Ten or twelve people had arrived ahead of us, including Arnie and Meg. Arnie was holding a small plate so full of food it was falling off the edges. Meg waved to us to come stand with them.

We did, and Arnie danced with each of us. It's not easy dancing with someone who's six feet five inches tall—especially when you're not quite five feet tall yourself. But it was good practice. As it turned out, I was glad to have it, because my last dancing partner of the evening was even trickier.

About the time we were done dancing with Arnie, my father came in with Mona. I think it was an official date. The way they giggled and carried on you would have thought they were back in high school. Mona was wearing a black dress with almost no back.

Shortly after the two of them came in, Dad walked over and asked me to dance. That was fun. The two of us dance at home sometimes, and we're pretty good at it. Then he asked Chris for a waltz and left me standing with Mona.

"So have you been thinking about my offer?" she asked, handing me a glass of punch. "Or have things been too hectic?"

I shook my head. "I've been thinking," I said. "I guess I'd like to give it a try."

"Good," said Mona. "I think it's going to be a terrific book. Besides, it will give you guys an excuse to come and visit me!"

I looked at her. She smiled.

What the heck? I thought to myself. *Dad could do a lot worse.*

I smiled back.

All in all, it was a pretty good dance. In fact, from Baltimore's point of view, it was wonderful. The articles about the treasure in that afternoon's papers had brought out a huge crowd. "This is it, girls," he said at one point, sitting down next to us. "This is the break we needed to get people coming back here. We're going to make this inn work after all!"

I thought that was nice, since it meant he would be able to pay my father, which meant my part of the finder's fee Chris and I would get for locating the treasure could stay in my college fund where it belonged.

But even with all the good news, it was basically a grown-up dance. So we found it a little dull, at least until just before midnight, when Captain Gray floated into the room and asked me to dance.

Actually, he didn't ask me in so many words. He just stopped in front of me, held out his arms and smiled.

I don't care if he had been dead for a hundred and twenty-five years. Who could resist an offer like that? I stood up and put out my arms. He took my hand in his. Even though it wasn't really there, it seemed as if I could feel it, cool and firm against my palm.

The music started, and we began to dance. It was like magic. A ghost can't lead, of course; he can't tell you where to go with just a bit of gentle pressure on your hand or your back. But I knew, anyway, knew exactly where to turn, where to move. It was as if he was telling me with his eyes, which were locked on mine. And it was as if I was seeing another time through his eyes, because even though I was still in the room at the Quackadoodle, at the same time I was back in Charleston, a hundred and twenty-five years before. I saw the Quackadoodle, and I saw another room, filled with dashing officers in gray uniforms and beautiful women wearing long, elegant gowns—and I was sweeping around that room in the arms of Captain Jonathan Gray, the most handsome man in the state. Even though I was wearing a modern dress, I could feel the layers of crinoline rustle around me as my long skirts whirled and whirled while we danced.

The people at the Quackadoodle must have thought I was crazy. I didn't care. It was wonderful, wonderful, wonderful.

And then the music ended, and Captain Gray took me to my seat. Then he put out his arms to Chris. A good thing he did, too, or she would never had forgiven me!

It was wonderful all over again, because as I watched, I still felt as if I was in two places at once.

And then the music was over. Chris sat down beside me. The ghost stood nearby. He had a distant look on his face. I could sense his sadness, and I wondered what was wrong.

"Maybe he thought he could leave after the treasure was found," whispered Chris.

That made sense. Ghosts are supposed to be restless spirits, tied to this world by some unfinished problem. With the discovery of both the treasure and the will, Captain Gray's problem seemed to be finished.

"I wonder why he's still here," I whispered back.

Chris shrugged. "Maybe he doesn't know the way home."

And then the clock struck midnight, and it didn't matter anymore whether Captain Gray knew the way home or not, because someone had come to get him.

Chris was the first to see him. She grabbed my elbow in the usual way and pointed to the entrance to the dining room, where a man stood, looking around the room and smiling.

I've never seen so much sorrow and so much joy wrapped together in one face. I've never seen such eyes.

I recognized him at once, of course. It had only been a day since Chris and I had stood in his house and looked at his garden, his bed, his papers.

It was Samson Carter, come to take Johnny Gray home.

He floated across the floor, weaving between the dancing couples, a smile as big as Christmas on his face. Captain Gray turned and saw him, and I could feel his burst of joy in my own heart.

Captain Gray nodded. Samson Carter nodded back, and put his hand on Captain Gray's shoulder. Side by side the two men turned to leave.

Chris and I followed them across the dance floor, through the lobby, onto the porch.

That was as far as we went, because it was clear the rest of the way was a path we could not travel.

Samson Carter put his arm around Captain Gray's shoulder. Together the two men stepped off the porch. They continued walking, rising higher into the night air with every step they took.

I had never heard a ghost speak before. But now I heard one sing—not with my ears, but somewhere deep inside me. It was Samson Carter. His voice was deep and rich and low, and its powerful tones filled me with the old, sweet song that had been a cry for freedom for his people: "Swing low, sweet chariot, coming for to carry me home." The words seemed to burn inside me. I thought my heart was going to split in two.

I watched as the two men crossed the lawn, their forms fading from sight with every skyward step, until there was nothing left but the mist and the final note of that old song. Then even that was gone, and Chris and I just stood there, staring and listening, our faces soaked with tears.

I have never been so happy in my life. And I knew, deep inside, that I would probably never receive a gift that would match the privilege of being allowed to watch the last run of the Underground Railroad, when Samson Carter came back to guide one more soul along the Glory Road to freedom.

"Swing low, sweet chariot, coming for to carry me home."

Good luck, Captain Gray, wherever you are.

ABOUT THE AUTHOR

BRUCE COVILLE is the author of dozens of books for young readers, including *My Teacher Is an Alien, Goblins in the Castle,* and, of course, the Nina Tanleven ghost stories. He has also written short stories, magazine articles, poems, an adult science fiction novel, and three musical plays for young audiences. His love of theater is part of what prompted him to write the first Nina Tanleven book, *The Ghost in the Third Row.*

Before becoming a full-time writer, Bruce worked as a teacher, a toymaker, a magazine editor, and a gravedigger. Now he is a frequent speaker in elementary and middle schools around the country and a sometime storyteller. Every once in a while he even gets paid for acting.

Like Nina, Bruce lives in Syracuse, New York. Unlike Nina, he is married and lives with his wife (and frequent collaborator), children's book illustrator Katherine Coville. Bruce and Katherine share their old brick house with a varying number of children, three cats (Spike, Thunder and Ozma) and a dog named Booger.

The dog's name was not Bruce's idea.